CW01590163

PEDICURES & PREJUDICE

BEAUTY SECRETS MYSTERY 4

STEPHANIE DAMORE

PINK SAPPHIRE PRESS

Pedicures & Prejudice

Stephanie Damore

For the dreamers and believers.
Keep being you.

1

The helicopter lurched forward and I swore for a second that Vince was up to his usual tricks. My bestie's husband was a bit of an adrenaline junkie. Causing his helicopter to take a dip would be just his idea of fun. But then there was rattling. And the power went out. I would never forget the all-out panic that filled me as we continued to race toward the ground. Hysteria. That's the word I'd later use when recalling the crash. I may have screamed. I know Aria did.

Instinctively I reached for Finn's hand. He clasped his hand firmly with mine and with my other hand I braced for impact on the roof of the cabin. My feet were pushed into Vince's seat in front of me. I squeezed my eyes shut as our aircraft made its rapid descent.

Sweet sugar, this is how it's going to end. I was going to die in a helicopter crash in the desert.

Finn's grip on my hand tighten. I turned and opened my eyes, staring hard into his. His gaze was just as intense.

"I love you," he said.

At least I think that's what he said. It was hard to make

out anything over Aria's screams. It didn't matter. I didn't need to hear the words to know that my only regret in life was that I hadn't had a chance to marry him.

The helicopter swooped and swirled out of control. Vince fought to steady the aircraft.

"Hold on!" he yelled, followed by some additional words in Spanish. Trust me, I was holding on as tight as I could.

Aria screamed right until the moment the helicopter crash landed in the brush.

"OOF!" My body was thrown hard and pitched forward, where it remained, saved by the five-point harness that I clung to like a kid on a roller coaster ride. "Get out, get out, get out," was all I could say. I kept thinking we needed to escape the fuselage before something catastrophic happened, like an explosion. Not a rational thought, but I couldn't blame my brain for thinking that way. My fingers couldn't work fast enough to unbuckle myself.

"I got you, babe." Finn was quicker than I, having escaped his harness in less than five seconds, and he helped me undo mine in a hot second. Vince apparently had done the same. I saw him kick Aria's door open, jump out and turn around to help his wife down. Finn and I followed route and managed to safely climb out of the aircraft and stumble after them in the desert.

"Guys, everyone okay?" Finn asked, taking inventory of the group. I looked at my arms and legs as if seeing them for the first time. Miraculously, I was unharmed.

"Vince, your eye," Aria said, her voice hoarse from all the screaming.

Vince's face had pretty nasty-looking gash above his eye, splitting his eye brow. Aria went to raise her arm to brush his hair out of his eyes and winced.

"What's wrong?" I asked.

"It's just my shoulder." I could already see a bruise forming on her bare shoulder from the impact of hitting her right arm on the door when we crashed. In fact, I was sure we'd all be sporting a few bruises, but I would take that any day over what could have been. Aria burst into tears and I knew how she felt.

My Nana in heaven was one busy guardian angel. With one hand holding Finn's, I reached up with the other and squeezed the cross around my neck, closing my eyes and letting out a deep exhale of gratitude.

I looked over at my bestie. Vince was doing his best to calm her down, but she was getting more worked up by the second. I struggled with a way to help, feeling much the same—overwhelmed. I turned to look at Finn. He had something else entirely on his mind. He wrapped me in the most tender hug and I was sure he would never let me go.

"I thought that was it, babe," he said, kissing the top of my head. I squeezed him a little bit tighter.

"I know." I would have liked to stay that way, but the fact remained that we were standing in the middle of the Mojave Desert with a crashed helicopter and my hysterical best friend. I gave Finn an extra squeeze and lifted my chin to kiss him softly on the lips before letting go of his embrace.

"The girl, the girl, the girl." Aria stammered.

"What girl, sweetie? I'm right here. Amelia's back home." Amelia was Vince's six-year-old daughter, but that's not who she was referring to. In fact, she wasn't referring to me either. Aria pointed at the scrub brush right besides us. I spotted the brightly-patterned bag first. It looked like a purse, or maybe an overnight bag. I dropped Finn's hand and took a few steps closer and wished I hadn't.

Sweet sugar, the bag belonged to the body of a woman. She was sprawled out face-first on the desert floor. Thick red blood clotted her hair, and a bloodied rock lay just in front of her. There was no point in rushing to her aid. In fact, I took a couple steps back.

My first instinct was to reach for my cell phone and call the police. But my cell was in my purse, which was still back at the helicopter, and I really didn't want to go back and search for it. I shudder to think what would happen if the entire thing blew.

Fortunately, Finn had carried his phone in his back pocket; however, the way he started to walk around in a circle told me there wasn't much hope for a signal. And Vince was focused on trying to get Aria to calm down. Unlike me, this was Aria's first time finding a dead body.

"What do we do?" I said to Finn. We had to alert the authorities about the poor dead girl, and our fate wouldn't be much better if we didn't find a way out of this barren land.

I knew it was a bad idea when Vince offered to take us for a ride. I should have listened to my instincts and not the tourist operator's enthusiastic assurance. Something tells me his opinion was heavily swayed by the wad of cash in his hand.

Finn motioned with his head toward the base of the foothills, where another type of smoke rose steadily into the air. "What about that over there?" he asked.

It was hard to tell for certain, but if I squinted hard enough it looked like an SUV with a tent set up beside it. Who would have ever imagined that anyone would readily go camping out here? Maybe I was more of a city girl than I thought. I could only hope that the people who were camping weren't the same ones responsible for this poor woman's demise.

Finn and I led the way with Aria and Vince trailing after

us. I noticed a sign marking the Valley of Fire Campground about the same time we noticed a couple of four-wheelers heading in our direction. In the twilight, the lights of the off-road ATVs bounced off the rough terrain. I thought back to the body in the desert not more than a quarter mile behind us and the lights riding toward us. First a helicopter crash, then a dead body, and now this? Vegas was not how I imagined it. I wondered if Vince's SOS calls had reached anyone before we crashed.

"How confident are we that they're the good guys?" I asked Finn.

He looked at the surrounding scrubby landscape, seemingly drawing the same conclusion as me. "If they're not, we're in trouble. There's nowhere to hide."

It didn't help that as the riders got closer, all I could see were bandanas covering their faces.

We instinctively stopped and formed a circle with our backs to one another. A protective stance. The riders stopped just before us. I turned my head away from the dust cloud.

"Y'all okay?" The woman's Southern drawl was music to my ears. She lowered her bandana and brushed the dust out of her hair.

"We saw your bird go down. Thought the worse," the second rider said, also a woman.

"We're okay. A little beat up," I replied.

"Do you by chance have cell service?" Finn asked.

"Already called for help," the first rider said. She held up a little orange and black device that looked like a walkie-talkie. These women were going to be my new best friends. As soon as we got out of here, I was sending them ginormous gift baskets and a lifetime supply of my Sugar & Sass products. Whatever they wanted, on the house.

"You guys want a lift back to our camp? We have a fire going for warmth and a first aid kit that can get that cut cleaned up. It's going to be a bit before the authorities can get here," the second rider said.

"That'd be great. Thanks, ladies," Vince replied, with a comforting arm around Aria. Tears still streamed down her face.

~

WHILE WE WAITED for help to arrive, the men downed plastic cups of whiskey and I devoured Irene and Eileen's chocolate stash. It turned out that our new heroes had a bit of a sweet tooth. It was the perfect remedy to a day that had spiraled completely out of control, literally.

We were sitting around the fire when the park ranger arrived. Being closest, he was sent to us first to assess the situation and see what additional help was needed.

"We received a distress call?" the ranger asked, looking around at our seemingly normal campsite.

"I, sir, our helicopter crashed," Vince said, standing and swaying a bit. I was thinking Eileen's hand had been a little heavy when she poured those drinks.

"Come again?" The park ranger asked, looking to the rest of us for confirmation.

"Our sight-seeing ride didn't go as planned and our helicopter made a crash landing. It's a couple of miles that way." I pointed in the general direction. By now it was way past sunset, and out here I could see the stars better than my own hand in front of my face.

"Is everyone okay?" the ranger asked.

"A little shaken, and somewhat stirred at this point, but

we're okay. We're just going to need a lift out of here," Finn said.

"Well that and the dead girl," I said casually. Aria flinched at the mention of the dead body. She had long since stopped crying and had spent most of the waiting time staring at the embers in the fire, refusing both alcohol and chocolate. Knowing Aria, my bet was that she was attempting to find some clarity of mind.

"Come again?"

"We found a dead body when we crashed. I think it's a woman," I clarified.

The ranger looked at me like I was joking. "You've got to be kidding me," he said.

"Trust me, it happens at an alarming rate with this one," Finn said.

"Dead bodies?" The ranger asked. Finn nodded, knowingly. The ranger assessed me in a new light.

"Thanks, babes," I replied to my beau.

"Anytime."

"Do you want me to show you where the body's at?" I asked the ranger.

"Nope, I'll take your word on it. I'm just going to call this all in and wait for the police to get here," he said.

"Now you know why they're drinking," Irene said.

"That I do," the ranger replied.

~

IT TOOK the detective just over an hour to reach us. The crime van and reporters followed in short order.

"Hi, folks, I'm Detective Hart. I understand you were in a helicopter crash and you found some human remains?" she asked. I liked that she was calm about everything, like this sort of business happened every day. Then again, she was probably used to some pretty whacked-out cases working for the Las Vegas Metropolitan Police Department.

No one else was talking, so I took the lead.

"We did. How about I show you where they're at? It's about two miles that way," I said.

"I'll come with you guys," Finn added.

"Hop in the SUV and you can lead the way," Detective Hart said.

"Where are we at exactly?" I asked the detective while she drove to the scene.

"About 50 miles northeast of Las Vegas. Lake Mead and the dam are just up the road." She pointed to her right. I nodded my head, trying to picture in my mind where that was exactly, but my sense of direction was a little fuzzy.

"Where you guys from?" she asked.

"Port Haven, South Carolina. We're out here for the Women's Leadership Conference. I'm scheduled to speak on Saturday. Thought we'd do a little sight-seeing first," I said.

"How's that working out for you?" Detective Hart said with a smile.

In terms of dealing with detectives at crime scenes, I'd have to say that this experience was one of the better ones. Detective Hart was more appreciative of us contacting the police than being accusatory. A nice change of pace.

"The body is right over here," I said before completely losing my mind. "Sugar!" I screamed, kicking my foot and stomping around. Detective Hart drew her gun and Finn stepped in front of me to shield me.

"What, what is it?" he asked, shining his flashlight along the landscape.

"Sorry, spider." Understatement. Make that tarantula. I'd

take a rattlesnake or bobcat any day over the furry eight-legged arachnid. As irrational as that sounded.

"I'm so sorry guys, it ran right across my foot," I said.

Detective Hart lowered her gun, and Finn smiled. I definitely was not liking Las Vegas one bit.

"This isn't good," Detective Hart said, bending down to look at the body. I imagined it wasn't. "Let me get some more information from you guys and then we'll get you out of here."

Neither Finn nor I said a word. That plan sounded perfect to me.

2

Despite the excitement from the night before, Aria and I managed to arrive the conference right on time the next morning. I might have been bright eyed, but I sure as sugar wasn't bushy tailed. In fact, in our attempt to be on time we completely bypassed the hotel's barista. Five minutes into the first presenter, I wished we hadn't. I needed my chai latte in the morning just as much as Aria needed her Sun Salutations. I was pretty sure she spent most of last night meditating given her Zen-like state this morning. Me? I was trying not to doze off.

And I would have if it wasn't for the hundreds of eyes staring at me. I was a keynote speaker, but I wasn't scheduled to speak until the day after tomorrow. Besides, I highly doubted that many people recognized me from the two-inch photo printed in the conference's literature.

"What is going on?" Aria asked me out of the corner of her mouth.

"You feel it too?"

"You mean like everyone is staring at us? Might as well live in a fishbowl."

"I know." At that minute, I heard a couple of people whispering and I just knew it was about us. I seriously couldn't stand it. "Let's leave right after this speaker."

"I'm good with that," Aria replied.

Forty-five agonizing minutes later, the woman finished her piece on *Demographic Changes and Their Impact on the Economy*. We stood to make our exit before the applause even ended.

"Ziva?" A woman stopped us just as we were about to escape through the conference room's doors.

"Yes?" I knew I didn't know this woman, who looked about as uncomfortable as I had just felt. Her brown hair was pulled back into a plain high ponytail and her eyes were magnified by a pair of plastic red-framed glasses that were far too big for her face.

"Hi, I'm Shelly Stevens from the Desert Sun Tribune? I was just wondering if I could ask you a couple of questions."

"About?" The conference organizers told me a few reporters would be on hand to gather publicity information, but I seriously doubted that's what Ms. Stevens was after.

"Um, I heard that you found Melanie May's body yesterday? At least I believe that was you at the crime scene," Shelly said.

"Lovely." That explained all the eyeballs. To think I had assumed the reporters weren't paying any attention to us. Rookie mistake. More than one person was waiting for me to answer. If my memory served me correctly, Melanie May was a fashion designer who was scheduled to speak at the conference as well.

"I'm sorry, but I only know Ms. May from the conference," I replied.

The young woman looked crestfallen. I recognized a girl boss trying to make a name for herself when I saw one.

"But if I do decide to release a statement, I'll give you a call."

Shelly's magnified eyes brightened. She quickly scribbled her number in a notepad, ripped out the piece of paper and handed it to me. I pocketed it, and Aria and I ducked out before anyone else could ask us more questions.

"What now?" Aria asked me when we stepped out into the hallway. A couple of heads snapped in our direction. *You've got to be kidding me.* I grabbed Aria by the arm and turned in the opposite direction

"Lattes. Big ones," I said.

We didn't stick around at the hotel, knowing others would be waiting to talk to us. Aria hailed a cab, not wanting to wait for an Uber, and we hopped in, instructing the driver to take us someplace for breakfast.

"Did you hear what she said?" I asked Aria. "The woman's body we found yesterday was Melanie May's." I hoped this morning's incident wouldn't cause Aria to have another mental breakdown, given how traumatic yesterday's experience was for her, but one look at her told me she was holding it together.

"As in the fashion designer?" she asked.

"Yes, as in the one who was set to speak before me at the conference." My mind jumped to all sorts of horrible scenarios, praying there wasn't some psycho on the loose targeting women in leadership roles. I thought about calling the guys, but there was no point. They were off getting their daily adrenaline-rush. One would think crashing in a helicopter would satisfy that for years to come, but not with those two. My only stipulation was that they didn't do anything involving aircraft.

"Even if we wear parachutes?" Vince had asked.

"Especially if you wear parachutes," was my reply. I

made sure to throw in a threat to Vince not to kill or maim my fiancé before our wedding. Sure, I didn't know any wedding details, as we hadn't been able to pinpoint exactly what type of ceremony wanted, but I could tell you that we would be getting married, soon.

THE CAB DROPPED us off at a greasy spoon and I was thankful it wasn't some up-and-coming fusion hotspot. Sometimes you just wanted a good stack of hotcakes and didn't care if it was served with bacon-infused maple syrup or vodka-spiked whipped cream. Aria would be satisfied with black coffee at this point, and I would take a mediocre cup of chai over having to deal with any reporters. We placed our order and while waiting I Googled Melanie May.

I could see why she had been invited to the conference. She was the epitome of a girl boss, and I felt an instant connection with her. While she was way more famous than I ever inspired to be, she had the same raw determination to build a brand that I saw in myself. Melanie's career took off when she focused on bridal fashion and a Royal donned one of her gowns for the big day. Since then she had been featured in some of the top designer magazines, and her work could be seen gracing the runways of only the fashion shows that mattered.

Naturally, the top news results on the Internet were focused not on her design work but on her death. I couldn't believe how many details and speculative articles had surfaced in the 12 hours since we had found her body.

"Did you know that Melanie had just gotten engaged last week to Zane Richards?" I said to Aria.

"Bad boy rock star Zane Richards?"

"Looks like it. The media's all in a tizzy; not sure if they should feel sorry for the guy or accuse him of murder."

"They did have a tumultuous relationship," Aria said. In fact, their rocky relationship was often tabloid news in itself.

I thought back to my mindless entertainment news knowledge and could vaguely remember a domestic abuse charge ... on her. "She was a bit of a fighter, wasn't she?"

"Zane called it *passion*," Aria said, using air quotes.

"Ah. Well regardless, it looks like the police have their first person of interest. Wonder if he's in town?" That question would remain unanswered because at that moment, our waitress brought out a ginormous stack of hotcakes for me and an impressive platter of sausage biscuits and gravy for Aria. My bestie shocked me with her order, forgoing her usual egg whites on wheat toast. I doused my plate in hot, sticky syrup with a slab of butter on top and waited for Aria's commentary, but she had already dived in.

"I see I've brought you to the dark side," I said.

"I just hate to think my last meal on this Earth would've been a quinoa bowl with steamed carrots."

"Now that would have been a tragedy."

"Is it weird that when I thought we were going to die my last thoughts were of food?" Aria asked.

"A little bit. Mine were of Finn. Well, the fact that we hadn't had a chance to get married yet."

Aria cocked her head in a knowing way. It wasn't a secret that I hadn't been able to make up my mind on anything other than the dessert table. "Any closer to knowing what you want?" she asked.

"Nope. One would think that after waiting this long to get married I'd know exactly what I wanted, but I think that's the problem. I've dreamed of my wedding day a hundred different ways and still none of them feel right."

"Not to mention the last time you planned a wedding, it was a disaster." Aria was referring to Mr. Ex-fiancé, who had recently married my archenemy slash friend.

"For the record, my wedding would've been fabulous. It was the groom that was a disaster."

"I'll give you that."

"But I think you're on to something. Maybe I do have a little wedding anxiety," I said.

"Hey, you remember what you told me when my wedding was falling apart?"

"That your first dress was hideous?"

"You did not!"

"That first dress *was* all wrong," I said.

Aria glared at me. "No, it wasn't about the dress. You said that as long as I was sure about the groom, the rest was irrelevant."

"I said that?"

"You did. And are you sure about Finn?"

"Absolutely."

"Well then, there you go. The details don't matter."

I licked the syrup off the back of my fork and thought that maybe Aria was on to something.

"What do you want to do now? Head back to the conference?" Aria asked after we both finished cleaning our plates.

"All those eyes watching us? I'm thinking no. Where are the guys?"

"Vince texted me a minute ago saying they were hitting up the motor speedway for some high-octane thrills."

"Yeah, no. I'm going to pass on that, too."

"Thank goodness. I don't think I could drive a race car in these heels." Aria glanced at me, but I was already clicking away on my phone. "This case is bothering you, isn't it?" she asked.

"It's just, Melanie was like us. A girl boss. She was just honored on Thursday night for a young artist award."

"Any sore losers?" Aria asked.

"I have no idea. I've already scrolled on. The speculations keep pouring in."

"Is there any legitimate news published about the case?"

"Not really. Police haven't even confirmed that was Melanie May's body that was found, which was probably why the reporter came looking to me for confirmation. It sickens me to think someone would just murder this bright young woman and dump her body in the desert," I said.

"I hear you."

"I'm going to step out and call Detective Hart." I reached to get some money out of my purse, but Aria waved me away. "Meet me outside?" I asked.

"Will do."

HERE'S the thing about Las Vegas: It's hot. I know they say it's dry heat, but ninety degrees is ninety degrees, dry or not. One would think I would be used to sweltering temps being a low country girl, but that desert heat was brutal. I swear I was going to need to chug my body's weight in water if I was going to rehydrate.

I dialed the detective's number and waited for our lines to connect.

"Hart," the detective said by way of greeting.

"Hi, Detective. It's Ziva Diaz from yesterday."

"Ziva, what can I do for you?"

"It seems that the body my friends and I found in the desert was someone famous, and the media has already connected us to the crime scene. I even left my conference early this morning because of it." The detective uttered a few choice, unladylike words, followed by a sigh. I imagined her closing her eyes and wishing she was magically somewhere else.

"So far, I haven't answered anyone's questions," I continued, but I was hoping you could answer a few of mine."

Detective Hart was silent, and I took that as a good sign.

"Basically, is it true? Did we really find Melanie May's body?"

Detective Hart was quiet for so long, I didn't think she was going to answer me, but she finally said, "We're not confirming anything publicly yet, but yes, you did."

I let the gravity of the truth sink in. For some reason, I liked the news articles better when they were purely speculative. "I have to tell you, this was the last thing our department needed," she added.

"How so?" I assumed a high-profile murder was never a good thing. Why should the timing be any worse now?

"My team's tired. Our murder rate is going up and for a city that runs on tourism, safety is everything. We have to clear this case, fast."

I took the detective's words as an opening. "I may be able to help. This is going to sound crazy, but I have a knack for solving murders."

"You what?"

"Trust me, I don't go looking for them, but I've walked into my fair share of homicide investigations and I've been able to close them all, quickly." Not to brag, but my track record was impressive. "I have references if that would help."

My girl, Detective Roxie, would be more than willing to add credit to my name—that is after she'd tell me how crazy I was for getting involved in another investigation.

"What are you offering exactly?" Detective Hart asked.

"It's more like, what am I asking for." I said.

"Fine, what are you asking for?"

"A chance to poke around a bit, see if anyone opens up to me. You'd be surprised the things people have confessed to me," I said.

"Listen, I'm not opposed to you asking around and seeing what you can find out—reporters do it all the time—but this isn't a two-way street. Don't expect me to be calling you with details. That's not how my department works."

"I understand."

"Good. If you hear anything though, I'd love to know."

"You'll be the first person I call," I said. Even as I said those words, I knew I was lying.

3

"I know that look," Aria said when she met me outside the diner.

"What?"

"You're taking this case on, aren't you?"

"How can we not?" I countered, deliberately adding the *we* in.

"Um, because we don't want to be the next dead body dumped in the desert?"

"And we don't want any other innocent women to be dumped in the desert either, now do we?"

Aria glared at me.

"You've got to quit looking at me that way. You know I'm right," I said.

"I don't know that," Aria replied. Now it was my turn to glare.

"C'mon. You know it'll be fun. Okay, maybe fun's not the right word. An adventure. It'll be an adventure. What do you say? Are you in?"

Aria looked down the sidewalk at the rows of casinos and neon. Something she saw helped her make up her mind. "Fine, but let me tell you, I liked this whole investigating thing better when you were the one finding the dead bodies."

"Don't worry, you'll get used to it," I said with a smile. Aria said something that sounded an awful lot like "don't bet on it," while I pulled out my phone and requested an Uber to pick us up.

"Where do we start?" Aria asked me while we waited for our ride.

"I was thinking we could do a little wedding dress shopping."

"I see you're taking my advice to heart," Aria said even though she knew exactly where I was taking this.

"Melanie's boutique is just off the Strip. Maybe someone there could point us in the right direction. That is, unless you know how to interview a rock star?" I knew if I was going to head up this investigation, sooner or later we'd have to secure some face-time with Zane Richards. How that was going to happen I had no idea.

Our driver dropped us off in front of Melanie's bridal salon. My heart sank a little when I saw the closed sign in the front window and the darkened interior. There was no point in trying the door. Maybe this case wasn't going to be so easy after all. For some reason, I thought we'd waltz into the bridal salon and get some grand clue that would solve Melanie's murder in a heartbeat. What can I say? I'm an optimist.

"Now what?" Aria asked.

"Not sure." I had searched Zane's website and social media channels on the ride over to see if he had any plans for the evening that we could crash, but all of his feeds were silent. Not even a tweet about his fiancée's passing. I wondered if there was a way to get in touch with his publicist. What I would say to him or her when I did was yet to be determined.

Our driver had pulled away and I was about request another one when the door to the bridal salon opened.

"Girl, look at that." From the khaki pants and button-up polos, my guess was that two plainclothes cops had just left Melanie's salon.

"Here, follow my lead," Aria said before anyone could come and lock the door behind the detectives.

"I'm so sorry," Aria said, as we stepped through the door. "I know you're closed, but is there any way we could just take a quick look at that little number over there?" By little number, Aria meant the elaborate feathered ball gown that stood front and center on the salon floor. I was pretty sure someone could get lost in all of those feathers. I was also very sure I would never be caught dead wearing a dress like that. But Aria was smart. I'd bet any money that dress was priced in the four-figure range, and there was no way a consultant could resist making that type of sale, especially when the right client walked through the door.

The woman hesitated ever so slightly before saying, "I suppose that would be all right." She flicked a light on over the showroom's floor. The gown glowed from the light above. "Do you mind locking the door behind you? I'm the only one here," she added.

"No problem," I said.

"Thanks so much for letting her try it on. We took a special trip out here to shop for a wedding dress. Ziva really wanted to try on one of Melanie's gowns."

I pumped my head up and down, not trusting myself to speak. All I kept thinking was, please tell me those feathers are synthetic. If not, there were a lot of naked chickens running around town.

The consultant flicked on some more lights. "So Ziva's the bride, I'm Gwen, one of the principal designers, and you are?"

"Aria."

"Nice to meet you both. Why don't you ladies follow me, and I'll get you situated."

"Excellent," Aria replied. I was still mute. Truth be told, now that more lights were on, I was eyeing up the shop looking for clues. However, the blush-colored carpet and brushed-suede ivory couches didn't offer up any forensic evidence. I wondered where Melanie's office was.

I didn't have a chance to explore as Gwen led us toward the back of the salon and deposited us in a mirrored fitting room along with the awful-looking dress. I looked down at my attire. I had not been prepared to try on wedding gowns.

"Forget your shoes. It's that black bra that's not going to look pretty," Aria said.

I ignored my bestie, suddenly struck with a flutter of nerves. "This is the first time I've tried on any dresses," I said.

"And it only took a murder investigation to get you motivated. That is so you," Aria replied.

"This is nerve-wracking," I said, pulling the heavy feathery fabric over my head.

"Fun, isn't it?"

"I don't even like this dress!" I hissed once the gown was properly on.

"Talk about hideous," Aria replied.

I would have responded, but I was dealing with a little bit of sticker shock. "Nine thousand dollars? Are you kidding me?" Apparently, I wasn't as cultured as I thought.

"Sshhh, don't let Gwen hear you."

I kept my voice low. "For all we know, Melanie was

murdered over a wedding dress, as expensive as these gowns are."

"Is it fitting okay?" Gwen asked through the door.

"Yes, we'll be right out," Aria hollered back.

I stared at myself in the mirror. I looked like Big Bird with white feathers. I doubted this was the vision Melanie had in mind while designing this gown. The top was gaping, the middle too tight, and the bottom made my butt look bigger than a hippo's.

I swallowed my pride and stepped out of the fitting room.

Gwen couldn't hide her appalled expression. I stood on the carpeted pedestal anyway and let her fluff out the dress while she stumbled over her words. "It's, um ... you look ..."

"It's okay. I know the dress is all wrong. I just really wanted to wear one of Melanie's designs. They look so beautiful on the runway." That last part was a lie. I had never seen one of Melanie's dresses before today. Well, unless you counted my Google search this morning.

"Just because this dress isn't the one doesn't mean we don't have a dress here for you," said Gwen, recovering her composure.

"Not to be insensitive, but do you know if you guys will be taking any custom orders?" Aria asked.

It was the wrong thing to say. Gwen, the model of professionalism this entire time, burst into tears. I was ready to bolt, wearing the ugly dress and all. Aria looked at me as if to say *oh no!*

Do something! My look said back to her.

"Hey, it's okay. I'm so sorry. I shouldn't have even asked." Aria wrapped Gwen in a giant motherly hug.

"She can't be gone. She just can't." Gwen sobbed on Aria's shoulder, and I eyed the distance to the fitting room.

"It's okay, sweetie. It's okay," Aria repeated.

"She was my best friend. I just—" Gwen broke down to the point where she could no longer speak.

I closed my eyes and tried wishing the crying heebie jeebies away. When it didn't work, I put my discomfort aside and stepped down from the pedestal to help Aria calm Gwen down.

"I'm very sorry for your loss," I added in, rubbing Gwen's back. The girth of the gown made it impossible for me to get any closer, but I did my best.

"I don't want to believe it," Gwen said.

That part I could understand. If something happened to Aria, I'd probably spend the rest of my life in denial.

"The girls are having a candlelight vigil tonight at the salon. It's so hard." Gwen wiped her eyes with the back of her hand. I dashed off to find a tissue. Luckily, they had boxes of tissues on every end table. I'm thinking a lot of happy tears were spilled around here.

"Her life seemed so bright. Any idea what happened?" Aria asked.

Gwen dabbed her eyes and took a steadying breath. "I have no idea who would've wanted to hurt her. She was kind to everyone."

"When's the last time you saw her?" I asked.

"Wednesday night. We went out to celebrate after the award ceremony. I dropped her off at home around 1 AM. I texted around 1:45 AM to tell her I was home. She texted me back *Good night* with a yellow heart." Gwen brought out her phone and showed us. Sure enough, Melanie texted her back at 1:42 AM.

"Did you see anyone suspicious while you were out or hanging around her place?" Aria asked.

"No, no one stands out. The police asked me the same thing."

"What about Zane? Was he in town?" I asked.

Gwen rolled her eyes. "Who knows with him. I haven't even talked to him. In fact, when Melanie didn't show up to work Thursday morning, I figured he had swept her off somewhere. He was always doing that. Missing important events and then popping in and whisking her way somewhere exotic."

"He used his money to show his love," I said.

"All the time."

I thought back to the price of the gown I was wearing. "You haven't had any crazy, irate customers lately, have you?" With the recent publicity surrounding Melanie and her young artist award, the accolades could have been the catalyst that set an irate customer off. Especially if they felt wronged somehow and were out big bucks as a result.

"Oh my gosh!" Gwen's hand shot up to her mouth. "Lucia. I didn't even think of her. She said Melanie would pay."

"Who's Lucia?" Aria asked.

"One of our clients. She came in about three months ago to have a dress designed. She spared no expense with her fabric selection and hand-sewn details." Gwen held up her hands and wiggled her fingers. "I spent days on that gown. Add in the number of design revisions and you're talking a price tag of close to twenty thousand dollars."

"Twenty thousand?!" Big Bird's price tag no longer looked so bad. "I'm guessing she never came to pick up the dress?"

"No. That's the thing. She dropped off the face of the Earth. We tried to get a hold of her for weeks. Melanie left messages reminding her that she'd be charged the full price of the dress, but Lucia never called back. Well, that is, not until we charged her credit card."

"I bet that didn't go over well," Aria said.

"It didn't. She came in irate, demanding we refund the charges. Melanie showed her in the contract where it stated that custom-designed dresses were nonrefundable and that payment would be charged in full two weeks after completion."

"But she didn't care," Aria said.

"No. She left the dress here and swore that Melanie would pay."

"What did Melanie do?" I asked.

"As far as I know, nothing. The dress is still here."

"Can we see it?" I asked. I doubted the dress had any clues on it, but I couldn't resist seeing what a twenty-thousand-dollar wedding dress looked like.

Gwen led us to Melanie's office. I had to turn sideways to squeeze through the door, feeling completely ridiculous. Pretty much the exact opposite way I wanted to feel when wearing my wedding dress. I looked around Melanie's office and decided that I immediately liked her style. Her office was decorated in shades of soft blues and yellows, highlighted by a painting that hung behind her desk. The artwork drew me in. Done in impressionist-style, it was a young girl with long, dark hair, spinning in a field of white wild flowers. The sky was blue and the day was sunny.

"That's beautiful," I said, looking at the painting to spot the artist's name, but it wasn't signed. Gwen agreed with a nod and turned our attention to the dress.

"Here it is," she said.

I'm not sure what I expected. One would think an expensive gown like that would be hung someplace more secure, maybe in a vault or at least in a closet with a lock, but the heavily beaded gown was hanging in a bag on a hook on the back of Melanie's office door. Lucia's phone number and name were stapled to the bag. I eyed Aria, letting her take the lead.

"Forget the artwork, this dress is absolutely beautiful," Aria said.

I reached out and touched the dress through the bag. Soft layers of lace and tulle were embroidered with thin gold thread and embellished with thousands of crystal and beads, creating a vintage-inspired masterpiece.

"Thank you. I'm pretty proud of it," Gwen said.

"This is your work?" I asked.

"Yes, and like I said, it took days." I couldn't imagine the amount of hand-sewing Gwen did. The dress had to be extremely heavy with all the embellishments, but Aria was right. It was absolutely beautiful. I was dying to get out of this joke of a dress and try that one on. Lucia's dress had thin spaghetti straps with a deep V in the front. I was betting it would hug my curves perfectly. "You mind if I take a picture of it? It is gorgeous."

"No, not at all. You can even try it on if you want." In the back of my mind, I knew that would be a big no-no. Never try on a dress you can't afford. But that part of my mind wasn't making decisions that morning. I shimmied my way out of the office and tried not to knock over anything with my double-wide self. I had never been happier to be back in a fitting room in my life. Gwen didn't think anything of it, taking the plastic bag off Lucia's dress and setting the slip of paper with her information next to it. Taking off the first wedding dress felt glorious in its own right. I could safely check princess ball gowns off the list. And things with feathers; that was also not my style.

But this dress?

The minute she slipped the sheath wedding gown over my head, I felt like old Hollywood royalty. I had been wrong. The dress wasn't heavy at all.

"How did you do this?" I asked her.

"Trade secret," Gwen winked. "Truthfully, I designed the concept a long time ago. I just needed the right client to come in and Melanie's name to finally be able to make it."

"You two were friends for a long time," I said. It was a statement, not a question.

"We were. Since our early design school days. Both of us had big dreams and we promised we'd support whomever made it first. Now let's go show you off in this dress."

I allowed Gwen to parade me out in front of Aria, who was sitting front and center on the white suede couch.

"What do you think?" I asked. It was a redundant question. Aria had tears in her eyes.

"Oh no you don't, girl. You are not allowed to cry. I will turn around and march back into that dressing room if you so much as shed a tear," I joked with my bestie.

"That dress is perfect on you. Finn wouldn't know what to do with himself."

I smiled at that. The dress flared out ever so slightly at the bottom. It swished when I moved my hips from side to side.

"Here, try this on." Gwen fastened a pearl comb in my hair and secured a simple elbow-length veil to the top of my messy bun. My hair had never looked so glamorous.

I looked at myself in the mirror. Somehow, I was going to have to explain to Finn that I had found the perfect dress. It was only going to cost us about twenty grand. Maybe Gwen could give me a deal. That is, if Lucia didn't come back for it. Perhaps Gwen could refund Lucia's credit card, and I could snag the dress at a deep discount? It was something to think about.

I had Aria come with me back into the dressing room, under the pretense that I needed her to take a bunch of photos of me in the dress and that the lighting was brighter in there.

"We'll just be a minute. Aria can help me out of the gown," I told Gwen.

"Here, take a few pics," I instructed Aria. I happily turned this way and that. I really did want pictures of myself in the dress, but when we were done, I motioned for her to hand me her cell phone and quickly snapped a picture of Lucia's contact information on her purchase order. Aria looked up at me in surprise and I smiled. I'm sure she didn't know what to think.

We met Gwen back on the showroom floor.

"Thank you so much for letting me try on that dress. I do absolutely love it."

"You're welcome. I'm so happy someone does."

"Yeah, I'm not sure it's in my price range, but if you think of severely discounting it, give me a call." I handed my card over to her. She read my name and smiled. "I love your products."

"Oh, why thank you so much."

"I'll definitely give you a call. Who knows, we might end up liquidating the store." My heart felt heavy for Gwen.

"Again, we're both so sorry. Not to go back to Melanie, but if you think of anything else on that front, give me a call. We're all girl bosses here. I'll do anything I can to help," I said.

Gwen looked uncomfortable. "There is one other person that comes to mind, but I really hate to go there. It's all just a bunch of gossip."

"You'd be surprised how often gossip leads the authorities to justice," I said. Aria nodded in agreement.

"It's this other designer. He's a bit of a drama queen. He accused Melanie of stealing his sketchbook. Claimed she nabbed it last year and he can prove it based on her latest collection. He created quite a stink when he found out she was being honored."

"And who might this other designer be?" Aria asked

"Paul Frederick."

"I don't think I know him," I said.

"I do," Aria said. "His looks are really eccentric."

"Right. They are. He got his start as a costume designer, designing for most of the big ticket shows in town. He's new to bridal fashion, but he's carried that look over."

"You should really tell all that to the police," Aria said.

"You think?" Gwen asked.

"Definitely. You never know what little clues can crack a case wide open," I said.

"Okay, you're right. I'll do that."

"If you need anything, give us a call. We'll be in town through Tuesday," I added.

"I will. Feel free to come back tonight. The vigil starts at 7 o'clock. I have to leave here and run to get the candles."

"Do you need us to get anything?" Aria asked.

"No, it feels good to be doing something for Melanie. Even if it's only this."

"I understand. Maybe we'll see you tonight," I said.

~

Aria and I left and watched Gwen lock up after us.

"Do you really love that dress?" Aria asked me as we headed down the sidewalk.

"Yes, didn't you? I wonder if I'll be able to find another one like it." I was already picturing the look on Finn's face when I walked down the aisle in a similar dress.

"Then let's buy it."

"Ha, I know my business is doing well, but I can't drop that kind of cash on a dress. It's just too much."

"Then let me buy it for you." I immediately objected. "No, seriously, consider it my wedding gift to you," Aria said.

"A wedding gift is like crystal or china keepsake. Not a five-figure wedding gown."

"You absolutely know you'd do the same for me. Here, let me make you a deal. If you find a dress that you love as much as that one, I won't object and I'll buy that one instead. But if not, consider Melanie May's dress yours.

"You mean Gwen's dress."

"Fine. Call it whoever's design you want. Deal?"

I knew I wasn't going to be able to talk Aria out of this and part of me didn't want to. "Fine, deal."

With that matter settled, Aria and I kept walking.

"So, what's our next course of action?" Aria asked.

"I was thinking about doing a drive-by of Lucia's house and then going from there. Not sure how we want to handle that though. It's kind of tricky doing reconnaissance work from a taxicab."

"I was thinking the same thing. Let's rent a car. Something with style."

"How about something that blends in," I countered.

"Girl, you're in Vegas. Style is what blends in."

4

The car's navigation system took us away from the glitz and glamour of the Strip to a neighborhood where the rockscapes were more like over-grown weed-scapes, and more windows had metal security bars over them than didn't. A couple of the houses were abandoned, if the kicked-in doors were any indication, and it looked like others were in the middle of being flipped, given the over-sized dumpsters in the driveways and debris piled up at the curb.

"Lovely." This wasn't the type of neighborhood where you'd find a lot of young families playing in their yards or business professionals washing their cars. "Tell me why you insisted on the Mercedes again?"

Aria looked around nervously, and I knew she was rethinking her rental choice.

"Unless we have the wrong address, I can't see how Lucia could have ever afforded that dress," I said.

"Unless she was up to some illegal activity," Aria replied.

"Like drugs?"

"Maybe. It's a possibility."

"Let's do a quick drive-by and see if it looks like anyone is home." I read off the addresses until we spotted Lucia's house. The driveway was empty, but the front window drapes were open.

"Why don't you turn around and park across the street and I'll run up and check it out," I said.

"Sure, but make it quick. We looked like two lost tourists just begging to get robbed."

"Got it. Keep an eye out."

"No problem there," Aria replied. I got out of the car and jogged up the driveway. The front door looked like it used to have a screen door on it, but it had since been ripped off. The metal hinges were all that remained. I knocked on the dented-in metal security door and waited. No answer. Cautiously I peered inside the front window. Thankfully I didn't see anything but a mess. A laundry basket had been dumped out on the couch, and several pairs of high heels and magazines littered the floor. Beer bottles and crinkled-up chip bags were thrown about, adding to the clutter. But no dead bodies, which has happened before.

I turned back to Aria and motioned that I was running around back for a minute. I could see Aria's eyes bug out, but I ignored her, stepping off the front porch and running around the side of the house.

The backyard was a barren landscape. While her neighbor had maintained his backyard, everything in Lucia's was dried up and fried by the sun. The scrubby space was depressing and dusty.

I surveyed the back of the house. Of course, the back windows were just tall enough for my short-statured self to not be able to see inside. Where was a trash can when you needed one? The best I could find was a rusted-out metal planter filled with cigarette butts on the cement slab by the home's back door. I carried it over to what I assumed was the kitchen window. Flipping it over, I stood on the planter to boost my height and looked in the window.

Even with the added foot, I could barely see in, but it was enough. Like the living room, the kitchen was a mess. The sink was full of dirty dishes—bowls of half-eaten soggy cereal, plates with dried ketchup, and cups of curdled milk. A jelly jar had been left open on the kitchen counter with a butter knife still stuck in it. I hopped down and moved the planter down a window. This time I looked into a mess of a bedroom. Dresser drawers were left open. A half-packed suitcase filled with clothes and toiletries lay on the bed. Lucia had run out of time. The question was why? Had she murdered Melanie and needed to run? Or was she running for another reason? I wasn't sure.

"Mind as well go on in. She's not home." The old man's voice came from behind me.

"SUGAR!" I slapped my hand over my heart.

An elderly man chewing on his tongue spoke to me from his back porch. With his beige pants and white undershirt, he blended right in with the landscape. I was pretty sure I could outrun him if I had to.

"Any idea where she went?" I asked when I caught my breath.

"Mexico."

"She said that?"

"Don't they always run to Mexico?" The old man spit tobacco juice onto the ground.

"Any idea why?" I said, hiding my disgust.

"I'm sure you already know." The man said the words knowingly.

"Riiiight. Okay, well, I'm just going to skedaddle then. Thanks for the info."

"Anytime."

And skedaddle I did, making a hasty retreat back to Aria, who had the car idling and ready to roll.

"What did you find out?" she asked when I jumped in and motioned for her to step on it.

"She's headed for Mexico."

"You found that out by peeking in her windows?"

"No, I found out she's a bit of a slob and she left in a hurry by looking in her windows. The neighbor who busted me told me where she was headed."

~

"Hi Detective Hart, it's Ziva again. I have a name for you."

"That was fast."

"I told you I was quick. Her name's Lucia Ortega. She ordered a twenty-thousand-dollar wedding dress from Melanie and never came in to collect it. It wasn't until Melanie charged her credit card that the woman reappeared, bringing threats with her. Anyway, I stopped by Lucia's house, and her neighbor said she hit the road for Mexico." I didn't want to go into too many details about the state of Lucia's house. I'd leave the detective to form her own conclusions once she had a chance to check it out.

"What's her name again?"

"Lucia Ortega. She lives over on Cherry Street. The address is 8102."

"Cherry Street is no place for you to be hanging out."

"Don't worry. I've already left, but I wanted to give you a call right away and let you know."

"What's a girl who lives on Cherry Street doing buying a twenty-thousand-dollar wedding gown?"

"That's the million-dollar question," I said.

"My guys definitely didn't tell me anything about this. I'll check in with them. Thanks, Ziva."

I clicked off with Detective Hart and turned to Aria.

"Is our work done?" Aria looked to me hopefully. I wanted to say yes, but I couldn't forget what Gwen had said about the other designer, Paul Frederick. He had a competing bridal salon on the opposite end of the Strip. It was definitely worth checking out until the police pinned Lucia. For all we knew, she hadn't been acting alone, if in fact she was the killer.

I relayed my thoughts to Aria.

"Well, at least you'll get a chance to try on more dresses," Aria said with a smile.

I thought back to that gorgeous, beaded, form-fitting gown. My stomach did a little flip flop. I wanted that dress bad. One look at my face, and Aria knew it too.

"I told you you loved that dress."

5

Frederick's Bridal was slammed. And I mean slammed. I was shocked to see a line out the door and couldn't fathom why so many women would be rushing to buy a wedding gown today. We asked the girl in line in front of us.

"Mr. Frederick released his new collection today. *Duh*." Okay, she didn't say that last word, but she might as well have given the look she shot us.

"Oh, yeah, that's right. I can't believe we forgot. Thanks," I said.

"What do you want to do?" Aria asked me, surveying the long line in front of us.

"I'm thinking that maybe we could use the chaos to our advantage. It might be easier to get someone to talk if they don't think they'll be heard."

Aria shrugged her shoulders. "Okay, let's give it a try."

Two girls dressed in black and sitting at a long table draped in a white cloth were checking girls in as they made it to the front of the line.

"Who's the bride?" one of them asked us.

"She is," Aria replied for us.

"Do you have an appointment?" the girl asked me.

"Here's the thing. We were supposed to have an appointment with Melanie May, but when we arrived at the salon, it was closed."

"Oh, you hadn't heard?" The girl leaned toward us. "She was murdered Thursday night."

"No!" Aria and I said in unison.

"Yes, her body was found decaying in the desert." Technically it wasn't really decayed. Obviously, I couldn't correct the girl.

"Oh my gosh, Ziva, what if someone would've murdered her while we were in her salon?"

I looked at my bestie, horror-struck. "We can't go back there, ever!" I said dramatically.

"What are we going to do?" Aria looked at the girl to save the day.

She bought it.

"Give me just a minute and I'll see if I have a consultant free to work with you." The girl talked to someone through her ear piece. "If you could have a seat over there, Clarissa will be out with you in a minute."

It was more like fifteen minutes, but I wasn't going to complain seeing how swamped the store was. I quickly learned that it wasn't the new designs women were clamoring after, but the deeply discounted gowns from last season. Heaven help me. This wedding dress shopping was serious business. I found myself longing for the little wedding boutique in Port Haven and a king-size candy bar.

Clarissa was a leggy blonde with a blunt-cut bob and sparkling green eyes. "Sorry to keep you girls waiting. It's been a madhouse since we opened the doors," she said.

"No problem. Thanks for fitting us in," I said.

We followed Clarissa back to a fitting room that had a settee and two gray bergère chairs. Aria and I sat across from Clarissa.

"I understand you had an appointment with Melanie May this morning?" she asked.

"We did," I said.

"It's so tragic. She was a great designer," Clarissa said. I was happy to hear her speak well of Melanie. Having a sympathetic consultant could only work to our benefit.

"I know. I love her work, but Mr. Frederick's is great too," I said.

"He does have quite a style about him." Clarissa pointed to the framed magazine spread in the room. Mr. Frederick was dressed in a black tux covered entirely in matching sequins, complete with a top hat. He looked like a circus ringmaster.

"That he does. I'm excited to see what you find for me." I tried to muster up as much enthusiasm as possible.

That comment got Clarissa back on track to helping me pick out the perfect gown. "What is it you're looking for exactly? Ms. May's and Mr. Frederick's designs aren't exactly alike," she said.

"I'm really not sure. How about you show me your favorite ones and we'll go from there? It doesn't matter what collection they come from. I love some of his original dresses," I said. My hope was that she would lead us away from the crazy sale out front and toward the dresses more in the back.

"Okay, we can do that. Follow me and I'll show you a few designs," Clarissa said.

"Excellent," I replied.

"While you girls do that, I'm going to wander around and see what I can find on my own," Aria said.

I hadn't told her to branch off, but that was a good idea. It would be easier to ask Clarissa about Mr. Frederick if it was just the two of us.

As we walked through the store, I could see elements of Mr. Frederick's stage work in his dresses. He wasn't afraid to incorporate unconventional materials or colors, like his off-the-shoulder mint green floral dress, or the sheer bodice one we saw with a floaty organza skirt. I didn't see one plain Jane wedding dress in the bunch. I also didn't see anything that I liked, let alone loved, but I did manage to lead us to a relatively quiet corner of the store. I looked side to side before whispering to Clarissa, "You don't think Mr. Frederick had anything to do with Melanie's death, do you?"

"What?" Clarissa asked, seeming surprised by my question.

"While we were out front here, I heard someone say that that they had some big designer feud," I said by way of explanation.

Clarissa looked over her shoulder to make sure nobody was in earshot. "It's no secret that Melanie stole his designer sketchbook. Mr. Frederick said if you look at Melanie's designs this year they're almost an exact copy of what he had sketched last year."

"When did his sketchbook go missing?" Gwen had only said last year.

"Last spring, at the Paris fashion show. Someone gained access to his hotel room and trashed it in an attempt to find his book. He knew his designs would surface one way or another and was ready to fight Melanie when she boldly displayed them in this spring's fashion show."

"What did the police say?"

Clarissa did a double take. "The police? Why would he go to the police?"

"You said she stole from him."

"Yes, his designs. His ideas. There was no way he could prove it in a way that mattered to them. All he could do was go after her reputation."

"So, he did and now she's been murdered."

"I know."

"Is Mr. Frederick here?"

"No. He said he needed some creative downtime. He'll probably be back in next week." Either that or he and Lucia are kicking it in Mexico.

"You know that looks really suspicious," I said.

"I know, but Mr. Frederick's bark is worse than his bite. He likes to pitch his little fits, but I don't think he's ever gotten into a real fight."

"You don't think he's involved in anyway?"

"I wouldn't be standing here if I did."

"That's a relief. It would freak me out to buy a dress from a murderer," I said.

"I don't think you should have any worries there. Now what do you think of this one?"

"It's, er, pretty." If I wanted to look like a peacock.

~

WE LEFT Frederick's Bridal and headed back to our hotel to meet up with the guys. The conference should have wrapped up for the day and hopefully the police had publicly identified the body as belonging to Melanie. If that was the case, I assumed the reporters would no longer be looking to us for confirmation.

"That was exhausting," Aria said to me.

"Tell me about it. You weren't the one trying on all those gaudy dresses."

Aria laughed. "Those were pretty awful, but that's not what I meant. It's mind-numbing trying to piece all these clues together. I don't know how you do it."

"I've never thought of it that way. I guess part of me likes the challenge. Plus, I have a thing for making sure justice is served. Speaking of which, it looks like I just found a possible address for Melanie. You mind if we do a quick drive-by? It looks like it's on the way."

"No, I guess not. Just text the guys and let them know we're taking a detour. I know Vince said he was starving."

"I am too." Breakfast was hours ago.

Melanie's condo was less than five minutes from her salon, which made sense. No one liked a long commute to work.

"That has to be her place." Aria pointed to the townhouse on the end with the crime scene tape securing the parameter and a crime scene van parked in front. Various police personnel were on the property; add in the news vans with reporters standing around, and it looked like everyone was waiting for something to start.

"Hurry up," I said to Aria as she looked for a place to park. The door to the townhouse opened and the reporters were on the move. I recognized Detective Hart immediately. She addressed the cameras first by confirming that the woman's body found in the desert was that of Melanie May. The reporters began shouting questions to her:

"Have any arrests been made?"

"Are there any witnesses?"

"Do we know the approximate time of death?"

"If you can hold your questions to the end, I will do my best to answer them. Right now it's early in the investigation. We are starting to piece things together and will update the public as needed. At this time, there is no concern for public safety." I didn't know what evidence the police had, but that last statement told me that either Melanie's murder wasn't random, or that they had a person of interest already in custody. If not, I imagined they would be warning the public to be on the lookout and not let their guard down.

"Is anyone in custody?" A reporter asked, ignoring the request to hold all questions.

Detective Hart kept her answer short, "No, not at this time. Now if you would please hold your questions, a representative of Melanie's family would like to speak."

For the first time, I noticed an older woman, probably in her late fifties, standing off to the side behind Detective Hart. The woman was petite and slender, with the same rich brown eyes as Melanie. She started by saying, "I just want to give a brief statement. I'm Veronica May, Melanie's mom. I'm sure you all know that my daughter was my world and our family is heartbroken."

Veronica's composure started to fall apart. She took a moment to steady herself before continuing. "I would like to plead with anyone who has information about my daughter's murder to please contact the Las Vegas Metropolitan police department. An anonymous line has also been set up if you wish to leave information that way. Melanie deserves justice. We need that justice. It's all we have left. Please." Veronica stared into the camera, her face raw with emotion. I thought she was going to walk away, but instead she squared off her shoulders and added, "And Zane? I swear, if you had anything to do with my daughter's death, you will pay. That's a promise."

Veronica looked hard at the cameras. Aria shuddered. I stared shocked that Veronica would end her statement with a threat to her daughter's fiancé.

"Was your daughter afraid for her life?"

"Did she tell you Zane might hurt her?"

Veronica ignored the questions tossed at her, instead turning and walking back into Melanie's townhouse.

"What in the world do you suppose that means?" I asked Aria.

"She clearly doesn't like Zane."

"I'm going to assume that she's not on speaking terms with him, either. I mean, who does that?" I asked.

"I don't know if we can fault her too much. She just lost her daughter."

"You're right, but there's more to that story. A lot more. I'm not sure who we can get to talk, but I want to dig deeper."

"That's not surprising. I wouldn't expect anything else," Aria said.

I took Aria's words as a compliment. "Now I'm even more eager to track down Zane," I said.

"You and every other reporter and news outlet in the country. I'm not sure even you can pull that connection off."

"I know, but that doesn't mean I'm not going to try."

"Once again, I wouldn't expect anything else. Now can we go get something to eat?"

"Yes. Food first, and then I'm tracking down a rock star."

I just had no idea how.

6

I greeted Finn with a kiss on the cheek and sat down next to him. A tall glass of sangria was already set at my place setting.

"How was the conference?" Finn asked us.

I looked to Aria. I didn't know how much she wanted Vince to know. Guess I was about to find out. "We sort of played hooky."

"That doesn't surprise me," Finn said.

"What do you mean 'hooky'? Where did you guys go?" Vince asked.

"To try on wedding dresses," Aria quickly supplied.

I was right. She didn't want Vince to know we were sticking our noses in the murder investigation. He might have a bad boy reputation with links to the Mafia, but he didn't want his wife anywhere near danger.

"Really?" That got Finn's attention. "Did you find anything you liked?"

"May-be," I teased. I wasn't about to reveal any of my dream dress details, especially the price.

"Did you guys set a date yet?" Vince asked.

"Not yet, but we're getting close," I answered.

Finn's eyebrows shot up. "We are? You're full of all sorts of surprises this afternoon."

"Are you objecting?" I asked.

"No, not at all. In fact, I couldn't be happier."

"Good then. Now what did you guys do this afternoon?" I asked, deflecting the conversation. "Surely you must've done something brag worthy."

Of course they had. Did Aria mention the guys were racing Lamborghinis and Ferraris around the motor speedway? It was the *Supercar Experience*, and I was just glad I hadn't been a witness. Finn makes me nervous sometimes when he's just driving around town. He's the most distracted driver I know. Don't tell him I said that.

We spent the rest of lunch in companionable conversation, with me making sure not to mention anything about Melanie or the murder investigation, and Finn eyeing me, knowing something was up. It was harder to keep quiet than I would have imagined.

"WHAT'S THE GAME PLAN TONIGHT?" I asked the guys after our plates had been cleared. I had even eaten healthy by my standards—a chicken Caesar salad wrap and fries dipped in honey mustard. Remember, I said healthy by *my* standards.

Vince rubbed his hands together in excitement. "I wasn't sure if my connections would come through, but I scored us four ring-side seats to tonight's fight." Vince accented the statement with a fake jab.

"Fight?" I looked to Finn. He knew boxing was not my thing.

"UFC Championship," Finn supplied with excitement in his eyes.

"Awesome, honey!" Even Aria was excited about this.

"Is this a boxing match? Cage fight? What am I in store for?" And how much alcohol would I have to drink to stomach it? Watching people kick the crud out of each other made me jumpy.

"Steele versus Volkov," Vince said, as if their names clarified things.

"It's going to be epic," Finn said.

"If it's going to be epic, I'm thinking I need to get in a nap before heading out."

"That sounds like a pretty good plan to me too," Finn said with his trademark eyebrow raise. Oh brother. He was going to be pretty disappointed when he found out that I really did just want to take a nap.

We parted ways with Aria and Vince and headed back to our hotel room.

"Now that I've got you alone," Finn said playfully once we were back in the room. I let him wrap me into a hug. "Did you and Aria really go wedding dress shopping today?"

"Oh, that's not where I thought you were taking this."

"Oh, I'm taking it there. I just wanted to ask you that one question first."

"I swear we did, scout's honor. I even found a dress that I'm sort of in love with." I held up my hands to stop him from asking the questions I knew he was begging to ask. "I want the dress to be a surprise. I'm finally starting to be able to visualize our wedding day."

"I was hoping I could persuade you to head to the little white chapel tonight."

Here's the thing: I knew he was serious, but I couldn't. "I would, and I mean that. Except my dad is not here. I can't imagine walking down the aisle without him giving me away. That's a deal breaker."

"I'll give you that. Your dad is a pretty cool guy." For the record, my dad was the best. Where my mom was a perfectionist and, some would say, a bit uptight, my dad just went with the flow. After spending a lifetime with me, I don't think I could surprise him even if I wanted to.

"Don't worry, babe. I'll let you know when I'm good and ready to say I do. First I have a project that needs a little tweaking."

"Tweaking?"

"Yes, tweaking."

"Are you sure you don't mean twerking?" Finn swayed his hips side to side against mine.

"Ha, yes, I'm positive."

It would have been too easy to prevent Finn from asking me more about this afternoon had I wanted too, but unfortunately for him, that wasn't the case.

"Aren't you going to ask me what else we did today?" I asked.

"Oh, I already figured you were out snooping around and interviewing murder suspects." I wasn't sure if I should've been impressed or annoyed. I decided to stick with impressed seeing I was marrying the guy. I couldn't hold the fact that he knew me so well against him. "The question is, why be secretive with Vince?" Finn asked.

"I'm leaving that up to Aria. He'd probably fuel up the jet and fly her out of here if he knew what we were up to."

"Or discourage her from hanging out with you."

"I sincerely hope he wouldn't do that, but you're probably right. Maybe tomorrow you and I can head out, and Vince and Aria can spend some time together."

"What time are you scheduled to present again?" Finn asked.

"Bright and early at 8 AM. After that I'm free. I wouldn't

mind getting the chance to talk to Melanie's mom, Veronica. She basically threatened Zane during her press conference this afternoon. And speaking of Zane, any idea how to talk to him?"

"No, but spending some one-on-one time with you sounds like a good idea."

Since Finn had taken the job down in Tampa and we were doing the long-distance thing, it was understandable that he and I would want to spend some alone time together. I was slowly transitioning my Sugar & Sass store in Port Haven to my manager and psychic friend, Izzy. Meanwhile, securing the storefront in Tampa was taking longer than I had expected. The real estate market was hot. This left me in limbo, wanting to be down with Finn, but realistically it didn't make sense to make that move yet. Speaking of which, I should check in with Izzy and see how things were going.

"OH NO, NO, NO," Izzy said by way of greeting. Izzy had a way of sensing my energy as soon as our telephone lines connected. She once told me that whenever I found a dead body, it came across to her like a blast of cold air. I was betting that right then, she was feeling arctic.

"Well, good afternoon to you, too." Technically, it was evening there. The time change was really messing with me.

"My teeth are chattering. You found a dead body again, didn't you? Are you sure you don't want to try my good luck spell?" A while back I asked Izzy to look into how I could change my karma given my morbid string of bad luck finding dead bodies. Izzy had in fact delivered a positive energy ritual that she said would remove the negative energy from my life and with that, bring me a string of good luck. Seeing things had settled down, I never did partake. Besides, it all sounded like a bunch of hocus-pocus mumbo-jumbo and it really wasn't my thing. However, given the helicopter crash and finding Melanie May's body, I was thinking it wasn't such a crazy concept after all.

"Can you email it to me again? I'll take a second look at it." I know it had something to do with the phases of the moon and all that jazz. I had no idea if the timing was right, but I could give it a go.

"How bad is it this time?" Izzy asked.

I knew what she meant. "Fashion designer. Girl boss. Body dumped in the desert."

"That's horrifying."

"That it is." There was no point in asking Izzy to guide me with this case. She strictly dealt with the land of the living. I had already tried that last time. "Anyway, that's not why I'm calling. How's business? Did we ever hear back from Senses?" The luxury spa chain had been interested in trying Sugar & Sass's products in its spas. Since Senses was headquartered in Las Vegas, I was hoping to have a face-to-face meeting with its executives before flying home in a few days.

"We did. Does Monday morning work for you?"

"It should. Send me the details and I'll confirm with them directly," I said.

"Will do."

"Thanks, girl."

"No problem. And Ziva, you might want to cleanse your energy sooner rather than later."

"Got it. I'll add that to the list." Along with interview a rock star and solve a murder.

7

"Do you care if I run back to Melanie's salon? They're having a vigil tonight. I'm hoping to talk to a couple more people. Piece more together."

It was just after 6:30 PM, and we had a couple of hours before the fight. Finn was taking the nap that I had let him talk me out of, and I couldn't see letting the opportunity to work the case go to waste. Truthfully, it would've been smart to take a nap. Tonight was going to be a late night. The game plan was to watch the fight and then end the night at Wicked Spoon. That last part was my suggestion and condition for watching the UFC Championship. Wicked Spoon's dessert selection overflowed with scrumptious treats, like enormous chocolate-covered strawberries, Godiva cake pops, and the must-try gelato bar. I heard that sampling the rich, creamy frozen treat would make you think you've died and gone to Italy. Even better, they were rumored to offer a mint-chocolate flavor. If I held on to that thought, I could sit through anything.

"You want me to go with you?" Finn asked, picking his head up off the pillow.

"No, don't worry about it. I'll find out more by myself. I'm just going to take a cab over to the arena after, if that's cool with you?"

"Yeah, that's fine, if you're sure."

"I am. Love you." I kissed him on his cheek. "I'll catch up with you in a bit."

"Okay. Stay safe."

Can I add that this is another reason why I love Finn so much? He doesn't try to talk me out of things; well, not usually. There's something extra sexy about a person who accepts you for who you are.

~

I TOOK a cab back over to Melanie's salon. When I pulled up, about twenty or thirty people were already milling around. Flowers and white balloons were being left out front along with words of loss and love written on the sidewalk with chalk. Melanie's friends and the community felt her loss deeply. It took me a second to regain my focus. I've found that when working a case, I have to distance myself from the victim or else my emotions cloud my judgment. Scenes such as this made separating myself that much harder.

A couple of young girls comforted one another, and I wondered what their relationship was to Melanie. When the first girl walked away, I took it as an opening to approach the other one who was left alone.

"I'm so sorry for your loss. I was just wondering if there's anything you'd like to say about Melanie?" I was prepared to explain why I was asking, but the girl didn't need a reason.

"Melanie was an amazing person. She really was. She took me on as an intern and had been nothing but inspiring. I'm not sure what's going to happen now."

"Intern? Like a design apprenticeship?"

"I'm not an apprentice yet. This is for school."

"Gotcha. Is that something everyone does?"

"It they can. In general, the more internships you can secure, the better connections you have when you graduate."

"That makes sense. I think it's horrific what happened to Melanie. Working here, does anything jump out at you that you'd want the authorities to know?"

The young girl looked around, seemingly unsure if she should speak her mind.

"It's okay, I promise I won't tell anyone other than the police. I'm not a reporter or anything. Just a concerned girl boss helping the police generate some leads."

"Well, it's just, Zane couldn't possibly be involved, right? I mean he's a famous rock star and he totally loved her."

"Why do you think he might be involved?"

"It was Wednesday. I was working with Melanie in her office when he called. Whatever he said set her off. She said she was tired of caring what other people thought. She was living her life, her way, from here on out, or something like that."

"Where does Zane come into play?"

"It was clear that he didn't agree with her, which only angered Melanie more."

I nodded. "This doesn't sound like Zane was involved, but that maybe he was trying to warn her about something. Is that a possibility?"

"I guess. I really don't know. Melanie was extremely upset about it. Enough that I ended up leaving her office to give her privacy."

"Did you see her after that?"

"No, in fact that's the last time I saw her, ever. She was

crying and upset, and I didn't help her. I just walked away. What was I thinking?"

"That someone needed a moment. You did what anyone would do," I said. The girl closed her eyes. "Trust me. I would have done the same thing, one hundred percent. There's no way you could've known what was going to happen to her. And for all we know, Zane's phone call isn't even related."

Okay, it probably was, but I wasn't going to say that.

The young girl looked at me and I could see the guilt behind her eyes.

"You're not responsible for any of this, but I'll make sure the person who is sees justice. Promise."

The girl nodded and thankfully her friend joined us at that moment. I let her take over comforting her friend while I weaved through the crowd to the salon's front door.

Inside even more people had gathered. Gwen and her coworkers had set up a table where guests could pick up a white candle and sign a guest book. The somber mood coupled with the glittering wedding dresses created a stark contrast. The clashing atmosphere was a bit unsettling and truthfully, bizarre. It reminded me of the time that I was at a funeral on a Saturday afternoon. When church got out and the front doors flung open, drivers honked their horns at the crowd of us milling around on the steps, thinking we were wedding guests waiting on the bride and groom. The juxtaposition felt exactly the same.

I didn't want to disrespect Melanie, but I also couldn't pass up the opportunity to do a little bit of snooping around. I suppose I wasn't really disrespecting her, seeing that I was trying to solve her murder.

I assumed the police had already searched her office, or maybe permission hadn't been granted yet and they were still waiting on a warrant. Regardless, Detective Hart made it clear that she wouldn't be sharing any information with me. I was on my own, and if I was lucky, maybe I'd be the first person through Melanie's office.

I waited until the memorial service started. Gwen was reading a beautiful poem about a sailboat disappearing over the horizon when I snuck back into the salon.

The back hallway was darkened, but I remembered the layout enough from earlier in the day to know exactly where Melanie's office was. Her door was closed but unlocked. I felt the heaviness of the door from the dress on the back of it when I swung the handle inward, just enough for me to squeeze through. I shut the door softly behind me and locked it.

Without any windows, the interior of the office was quite dark. I took out my cell phone and tapped on the flashlight app to light my way. Obviously, it would have been way easier to flick on a light. Easier but not smarter. Nothing draws attention like the glow from an office door in a dark hallway.

The first places I thought to look were her desk and filing cabinet, possibly her laptop if I had the time and it wasn't password protected. The fact that her computer was still here was a good sign. That meant the police hadn't confiscated it yet.

The filing cabinet was filled with normal business papers—purchase orders, fabric catalogs, and employment applications—for the most part. I did find one folder titled "HR," but if I was looking for any disgruntled employees, I was out of luck. No one had even been written up. I did, however, find an employee phone number record that I snapped a picture of.

Next, I got to work on Melanie's desk. She was my kind

of girl. Her bottom desk drawer was like a convenience store ... candy bars, little bags of cookies, snack packs, with a wrinkled bag of ramen under it all. I could relate. The rest of her drawers were full of sketch pads, pens, a measuring tape, fabric swatches, color palettes, paint brushes, pretty much everything you'd except from a fashion designer. Nothing to help me solve her murder.

I turned my attention toward her computer and that's when I heard it. I wasn't the only person with the same idea. The door handle jostled and my heart stopped. I darted my head back and forth, looking for a place to hide, and dove under the desk. The person tried the handle again, this time more forcefully, but the door didn't budge. The woman cursed from the other side of the door. Guess she didn't have a key. Thank you, Jesus. I could only hope she wouldn't still be outside when I went to sneak out; that, and she didn't know where to find a key.

I stayed hidden for a moment longer and steadied my breathing. Now was not the time to freak out. With my composure regained, I put my hand on the underside of the desk to prevent myself from hitting my head when I stood up. As I did, my thumb made contact with an indent. It was a button. I pushed it and felt the drawer above my head give a pop. The fact that a hidden compartment could be contained within such a modern piece of furniture surprised me. I pulled open the drawer and saw a secret eight- by ten-inch compartment. Inside, it contained a small spiral notebook and a set of index cards.

I opened the notebook and, using the light from my phone, saw page after page of numbers separated by commas. I studied the numbers, counting the sequences. They were all the same. Nine numbers followed by another five numbers followed by another set of six numbers. I had no idea what I was looking at, but line after line repeated the same pattern. I snapped a few pictures of the pages and closed the notebook, making sure to leave it where I found it.

The stack of index cards was more straightforward. A sticky note had been placed on top of it, which read *These are the last ones. We're done.* Each note card contained a name and phone number followed by two or three dollar signs. I took some pictures of those as well and put the whole stack back, clicking the compartment shut. What did the numbers mean and who were the notecards for? I'd have plenty of time to put the pieces together *after* I escaped.

I said a prayer and opened the door. Whoever had been outside it a moment ago was gone. I didn't waste any time to see if they'd come back.

I detoured to the bathroom to give myself a moment to collect myself. When I stepped out, I practically walked right into Veronica Mays, Melanie's mom. The day had taken its toll on her or maybe it was the vigil. Regardless, based upon her looks, the press conference could have been ages ago.

"I'm terribly sorry for your loss. I've heard wonderful things about your daughter," I said.

"Thank you. I'm at a loss."

"I can only imagine. I know now's not the time, but I saw your press conference today and I want to help."

"How so?" Veronica looked at me skeptically and that was understandable.

"My friends and I are the ones who found your daughter's body after our helicopter crashed. I've spoken with Detective Hart and offered to lend my services, which she has agreed to."

"Services?"

"People tend to open up to me, and that leads me to get clues that the police would otherwise not obtain. With your permission, I'd like to stop over and chat with you. See if there's anything else you can tell me might help us catch Melanie's killer."

Veronica's sunken eyes stared off into the distance. "I suppose it would be all right," she said after a moment.

"Do you think tomorrow late morning might work for you?" I asked.

At that moment, Gwen interrupted us. "I'm sorry, Veronica, I just wanted to catch Ziva here before she took off," she said.

"What's wrong? What can I do for you?" I asked.

"Oh, nothing like that. I just wanted to say thank you for earlier today when I was a total mess. You and Aria were a blessing."

"You don't have to thank me for that, but I'm glad we were some help."

"You were and I hope maybe something I said leads the police in the right direction."

"I do, too. That's actually what I was just talking to Mrs. Mays here about."

"She's legit," Gwen said and gave me a one-armed hug. "I better get back. Feel free to give me a call if I can help again."

"I will," I waved bye to Gwen and turned my focus back to Veronica. "Anyway, do you think tomorrow morning would work?"

"Tomorrow won't, but I'm free now if you don't mind talking at my place. I need to let Mitsi out."

"Are you sure?" I didn't want to force my company on someone who clearly needed some rest.

"If you think you can help, I'd rather talk now."

I understood that. I looked at my watch. It was already after 8 PM and I should be heading to meet Finn and the gang, but this was more important. I made an executive decision. "I can do now," I said.

"Give me a minute to say some goodbyes and then we can go."

"I don't have a car, so I'll follow you in a cab," I said.

"Nonsense. You can ride with me. I trust Gwen."

I nodded my okay, not sure if that was a good idea or not. Veronica might trust Gwen, but did I trust Veronica?

8

I texted Finn on the way to Veronica's house. I would have called him, but seeing Veronica was in the car, that would've been a bit awkward.

Want me to meet you? Finn texted back.

No. I think I should interview her alone. Given her comments about Zane, I was betting she'd be more talkative one-on-one.

I thought we were going to spend some time together. Even via text I could tell Finn was annoyed.

I'll meet you guys right after. Promise. This shouldn't take long. I hoped.

Veronica lived in a lovely single-story home in an upscale neighborhood just far enough away from the Strip to be considered residential. She parked her Lincoln in the garage and we walked through the entrance into the brightly lit kitchen. Mitsi turned out to be one ridiculously hyper, and yappy, Yorkie. The puppy wouldn't even sit still long enough for me to pet her.

"Let me put her outside for a minute so she can burn off

some of that energy," Veronica said, scooping up the puppy, who immediately started licking her face. As soon as Mitsi was outside, I could see her zip from one end of the yard to the other, barking the entire time.

"Coffee?" Veronica asked me when she returned. I was surprised she offered coffee when she appeared to have a variety of tea boxes sitting on her kitchen counter.

"Sure." Truthfully, I wasn't a coffee person, but Veronica was already working on making a pot and I didn't want to be rude. Plus, if it helped Veronica open up, then I would gladly sip on a cup.

Veronica's town house was decorated in shades of white. Framed dance portraits and paintings brought pops of color to her walls. My favorite was Degas' *Dancer*, which hung above her living room sofa. A replica no doubt. Given the painting in Melanie's office and the ones in Veronica's home, it appeared both women had a love for Impressionism.

I took a seat with my back to the painting while Veronica placed the coffee tray on the table in front of us and sat on the opposite side of the couch.

"I've had a chance to talk with Gwen, and I stopped by Mr. Frederick's salon to talk with his staff too, but I really wanted to talk to you about Zane. I heard what you said at the press conference. Could you tell me more about that?" I said as I doctored up my coffee. I mean I *really* doctored it up, with a heavy pour of cream and two heaping spoonfuls of sugar.

Veronica wasted no time answering my inquiry. "Zane kept her head in the clouds. Her feet used to be firmly on the ground, but whenever he came around she lost all common sense. I hated that."

"Had she ever let a man do that to her before?"

"Never. One thing I admired about my daughter was her ability to stay focused, stay true to herself. I like to think she got that trait from me."

I noticed a black and white photograph of a younger Veronica striking a ballet pose. "You were a dancer."

"Still am. I don't tour anymore, but there's enough work out here to keep me happy. Maybe not lead roles, but enough." Veronica got that distant look in her eyes once more.

"Back to Zane, why do you think he might be involved with Melanie's murder?"

"An instinct? He was jealous. Possessive. At times, I wondered if he really loved my daughter or if he just liked controlling her."

"Do you think he was physically abusive?"

"I wouldn't be surprised, although Melanie would never admit to such a thing. She was in love with him." Veronica was disgusted.

"Do you have a way for me to get a hold of him?" I asked.

"No." My shoulders slumped. No one knew how to reach him. "I've generally made it my business to not know where he is. The playboy has probably already flown off somewhere, like New York or who knows where, maybe even Paris." Veronica's voice became edgier. There was more there, but I didn't ask her about it. "I just can't believe my baby's gone. Why her? Why?"

There was nothing I could say except, "I'm so sorry."

Veronica curled her legs up underneath her on the couch. I could tell my questions had already taken their toll as had the rest of the day.

"I'm going to leave you to get some rest." I stood and retrieved my card from my purse. "I'll leave this here for you in case you think of anything else or if you want someone to talk to." I spotted a blanket folded on the arm chair in the corner of the room. I picked it up and covered Veronica's legs with it, urging her to get some sleep.

"Can I get you anything? Would you like a pillow or even a cup of tea?" I noticed Veronica's coffee sat untouched.

Veronica laid her head down on the couch's armrest and zoned out. "Perhaps just a quick nap and then I'll be able to talk more," she said, half asleep.

"Don't worry about me. You catch some Zs. I'm going to let myself out and I'll be sure to lock up." Veronica didn't respond.

I opened the sliding glass door to let Mitsi back in before leaving Veronica to recharge. I wished at that moment I could call someone to stay with her. I should have asked if she had any other family in town. I hated leaving the woman in such a fragile state with just a puppy to keep her company. Without another option, I sighed and walked out of her town house, making sure the door locked behind me.

I thought back to how Veronica looked earlier in the day. The woman with fire in her eyes and threatening words was replaced by a depressed mother with a distant gaze. The death of her daughter was too much. Veronica's mental state only made me want to solve the case even more.

~

I TOOK a cab to the T-Mobile Arena to meet up with the guys for the fight. Finn was waiting for me when the cab dropped me off. "How'd it go?" he asked.

"Good. I found out some more information on Zane. I can fill you in later," I said. The thumping of the music inside the arena picked up the moment we walked through the doors. Finn wouldn't be able to hear a thing I said once we were on the floor.

"You missed the undercard, but the main fight's about to start," he said, picking up the pace. I had to almost run to keep up with his stride. These short legs could only walk so fast. Finn turned and looked at me power walking to keep up. He slowed ever so slightly. One could say that Finn was a bit excited to get back to the action.

We walked through the ground floor entrance tunnel. The music beat thumped louder. Bright white spot lights danced around the darkened arena. The exception was the lit-up boxing ring front and center. Our seats were in section B, although no one was sitting.

"Girl, you made it!" Aria said, giving me a hug with one arm with a cocktail in the other. I smiled back, but my greeting wasn't nearly as enthusiastic.

Honestly, it was really hard to get into the atmosphere. I would've much preferred a quiet evening back at the hotel with a nice glass of red wine and a chance to process this case. That realization had me feeling totally lame and I did not want to be lame or a party pooper, as Mrs. J. would say. Mrs. Birdie Jackson was my surrogate Nana and the new Mayor of Port Haven. Whenever I was down in Tampa, I missed her home cooking something fierce. I also realized that she was hipper than I was. She would love it in Vegas. I decided in that second that I would try and have fun.

"Do you want a drink?" I asked Finn. If I was in fact going to make an effort then I was going to need a little liquid encouragement.

"Sure, but ..." I knew Finn wasn't about to leave our prime seats and I wasn't about to wait for a waitress to sling drinks this way.

"No, it's okay, I got it," I said, eyeing the tunnel back out. I remembered seeing some drink vendors right outside the door.

While waiting for a couple of rum and cokes, I looked around and thought, *Las Vegas is the only place in the world that consistently makes me feel underdressed.* Along with the over- the-top outfits, I've also learned that it's appropriate to be drunk at all times while in Vegas (Hello! They have daytime pool clubs!). I may not be one for professional fighting, but I could people watch all night long. The combination of the outfits and the alcohol gave me a plethora of eye candy. Neck-breaking high heels and cha-cha revealing skirts were just the start of it.

Then I spotted him.

Walking through the crowd, with lights flashing and girls chasing, was Zane Richards. A black blazer and dark jeans never looked so appealing. A leggy brunette was on his arm. I had no idea who she was, but having her there just added to the image. Seeing a rock star in all his celebrity glory was an experience in itself.

"Zane! Zane!" The paparazzi shouted, their flashes popping in rapid succession. Zane tossed the cameras a wave and one of his million-dollar smiles. Security cleared the way and led him right past me and through the tunnel I had just walked out of. I was about to cut out of line and follow, until my senses came back to me. No way would I be able to get close enough to touch him, let alone ask him a question.

Ten minutes later, I was walking back to my seat with two drinks, keeping my eyes out for Zane all the way.

"Did you see him?" I asked Finn.

"See who?" Aria hollered.

"Zane. He and his entourage walked past me while I was waiting in line."

Aria's and Finn's heads turned this way and that, but none of us saw him.

"Who are you looking for?" Vince asked.

"I thought I saw someone famous. I must've been mistaken," I said, taking a sip of my drink. What I had I just learned? That Zane was in town. That was a start.

9

Seven AM came mighty early, which meant I'd be sporting some serious jet lag when we flew back home. Too bad I couldn't stay on Mountain Standard Time. Finn had no problem getting up. He even ordered room service—chocolate chip pancakes for me and steak and eggs for him. One would think I'd never be able to eat again after indulging in more than a few desserts last night post fight. They would be wrong. I sampled it all. Some might say I'm a nervous eater. They would be right. I blew out a breath I hadn't realized I had been holding.

"Are you sure you don't want me to come down?" Finn kept insisting on watching my presentation, but I told him it wasn't necessary. I appreciated all of his support, but having him there would make me more nervous than anything.

"Positive. Trust me, it'll be super boring," I said.

"Babe, it's never boring when you're in business mode. It's actually kind of sexy." Finn advanced toward me.

"Oh no you don't. You're not distracting me with your hotness. I've got to keep my mind sharp right now."

"I can be quick. Ten minutes, tops." His fingers traced the buttons on my blazer.

"Finn Hudson!" I swatted his hand away. "I'm headed downstairs right now before you make me irresponsible. Don't forget you have homework to do."

His homework this morning was to see if he could find a way to connect with the rock star. Even knowing if Zane was in town and where he was staying would be a start.

"We'll see." Finn fell backwards on the bed, remote in hand.

"Oh, you're going to be like that again? How about you see what you can find out about Zane, and if you're a good student I'll let you be the teacher's pet."

"Can I pet the teacher?"

"Ugh! You're impossible!" I attempted to storm out, but the effect was lost due to my laughter. "I'll text you when I'm done. Hopefully it'll be before ten."

"Good luck, babes. Love you." I blew him a kiss as I walked out the door and skedaddled before he could make another move.

~

I SAW SHELLY, the reporter from the morning before, sitting in the front row waiting for my presentation to begin. Something told me that she wasn't there to take notes on branding. I gave her a smile to let her know that I recognized her and decided it was a good thing that she was there.

"Do you want to catch up after this?" I asked her in the minute before things were scheduled to kick off.

"Absolutely."

"Great." I was thinking the least we could do was compare notes.

At 8 AM sharp, I kicked off my spiel. This was just like running a beauty demo, which is why I brought free samples of my best-selling facial scrub and moisturizer to pass out.

During my presentation, I talked to the women about the importance of understanding market demands and how if you did your research and launched a product that fulfilled that demand, then the branding was the cherry on top.

"Just like with dessert, branding is what stops and makes you say, *Oooh! I have to have that!* Am I right?"

Of course I was. Anytime you could use dessert in an analogy, you had to be.

I expected a few people to ask questions afterwards. I did not expect the line-up nor the requests for autographs.

"Have you thought of writing a book?" one woman asked me by way of introduction.

Her question caught me off guard. "Um, no, can't say that I have. I'm not quite sure what I could possibly have to say."

The woman looked behind her at the line. "Oh, I'm sure you have plenty. Take my card; I have yours. I'll be in touch."

People wanted to know if I had any new products in the works, what advice I had for starting out, where I found my inspiration, and how I overcame self-doubt. I had to laugh at the last question.

"Self-doubt. Well here's the thing. I didn't set out to create a natural skincare empire. I set out to make products that I would love and that I could share with my friends. The rest snowballed. So you see, there wasn't time for self-doubt."

Finally, finally! The line was gone and thankfully Shelly had stuck around. I found her waiting for me outside the conference room.

"I'm so sorry about that. I had no idea the reaction would be that positive. Thank you for waiting."

"Absolutely. You were fantastic."

"Thanks so much." I swiped my bangs out of my face. "So, I'm not making any official statement, but if you're interested in grabbing a latte and swapping notes, I would be down for that."

Shelly didn't hesitate. "Okay, let's go then."

I know I said I was going to grab a latte, but we ended up back at Wicked Spoon. What can I say, their desserts were amazing. Plus, last night they had the most scrumptious looking macarons I had ever seen but I had run out of room to sample. The fluffy meringue cookie with buttercream filling would be the perfect reward for slaying my presentation. Plus, all the bright colors and flavors were absolutely mouthwatering—raspberry, lemon, chocolate, mocha, coconut, cherry—I wanted them all.

I ordered a sample flight for the two of us to split. No harm in mixing business with pleasure.

"I'm ashamed to admit, but I have the worst sweet tooth," Shelly said while debating which cookie to start with. "Have you ever had their molten chocolate lava cake here?"

"What? No. I didn't even see it!" I said, scanning the menu for it.

"Oh my goodness, it's heaven. It's a dark chocolate cake basically swimming in a pool of warm caramel."

"Are you kidding me? That sounds amazing." And like something I must sample before leaving town. I knew Finn would be down. He loved caramel.

"It's the best. I have no shame," Shelly laughed.

"I'm right there with you, sister. I live off sugar," I said.

"It's the best, isn't it? Especially chocolate." Shelly selected the chocolate macaron and I immediately regretted not getting two of that one.

"I love chocolate," I said almost wistfully.

"And chocolate chip ice cream," Shelly said.

"*Mint* chocolate chip ice cream," I said.

"Yes! That's the best. And chocolate-covered graham crackers."

"Those are my favorite! Did we just become best friends?" I joked.

Our conversation continued to go way off track, but I managed to bring it back around to the case once our drinks were delivered.

"I assume you spent yesterday asking around about Melanie's murder. Am I right?" I asked while sipping my chai latte.

"I did. You?"

"Same. Anything you're willing to share?" I asked.

"Well, it's nothing I'm sure the police don't already know, but my editor sure was interested. That is if I can prove the claims, which I'm working on."

I wasn't following. "What claims are you talking about?"

"How about you tell me what you've heard first, and I'll try to see where my story fits in."

"Okay, fair enough." I thought about where to start and how much to filter. I didn't need my speculations ending up in the morning paper, plus I had told the intern last night that her thoughts were safe with me. I decided to fill Shelly in on what I had heard about Melanie's feud with Paul Frederick, to which she nodded, as if she had heard about it as well. I also told her that I ran into Veronica, Melanie's mom, and that really got her interest.

"She was really that depressed?"

"Absolutely. I don't blame her, what with her daughter being murdered." I wasn't a mom but I could only imagine the pain she must be feeling.

"That doesn't jibe with the picture I was painted of her."

"What do you mean?" I asked.

"According to my source—"

"Who?" I interrupted.

Shelly held up her hands. "I can't tell you. Trust me I would if I could, but the information was given to me confidentiality. I'm going to keep it that way."

"Fair enough." I backed off.

"Anyway, my source told me that Melanie and her mom were estranged. In fact, they had spent most of their lives at odds with one another."

"Really? I didn't get that vibe at all."

"From what I heard, Veronica was a ballerina and she blamed her daughter for ruining her career. I guess the pregnancy came at the wrong time and she never hit it big as a result."

"So, Veronica resented her daughter." Come to think of it, maybe that was the vibe I was picking up from her last night. It was hard to tell.

"That's what I'm told. And the more successful Melanie became, the angrier Veronica was. I need to confirm it, but my source also said Veronica was suing Melanie over an alleged business loan. Veronica gave Melanie the money to produce her first collection, but was never paid back in full. Veronica was attempting to collect the funds with a vengeance."

"She was suing her own daughter? That seems like a bit much. How confident is your source?"

"Very. I can't give you the details, but I trust her."

"How much money are we talking here?"

"Not sure. I'm headed to check the court records to see what I can find." How much jealousy and resentment did Veronica harbor? Their relationship had to have been complex if at one time Veronica lent her a sizable amount of money. Plus, through it all, Veronica was still proud of Melanie. I picked that up yesterday as well.

"She was also angry at Zane for turning her sensible daughter into a lovesick fool."

"Veronica has issues with men in general."

That got an eyebrow raise out of me. "Does she now? Did your source by chance say who Melanie's father was?"

Shelly nodded her head. "Some Russian ballet dancer. That's all they knew."

"WELL, do you mind sharing with me what you find out? I'm still trying to track down Zane." Finn hadn't text me since I left. I assumed that meant he had struck out in his search.

Shelly snorted, causing her glasses to slip down her nose. "I'm sorry. Good luck with that one."

10

I was right. Finn had come up empty and was watching Sports Center instead when I called him.

"Hey, I talked to that reporter girl again and found out some more information on Veronica," I said.

"Anything good?"

"Possibly. I want to go back to Melanie's salon and try to confirm some of the details."

"Okay, just give me five minutes and I'll meet you downstairs."

"NO!" I shouted into the phone. "I mean you can't." Oh crud. Here I was blowing off Finn again. I had to tread carefully. "It's just, that's where the wedding dress is. I don't want you to see it."

Finn's tone changed immediately. "What's the name of the salon again?" Finn teased.

"You better not show up there!" I threatened. Finn was smiling on the other end of the line, I knew it. "This won't take that long and we can still play tourist when I'm done. Promise."

I hung up with Finn and gave the salon a quick call to see if Gwen was in. She was with a client, but she was there. That was good enough for me.

Ten minutes later, I walked into Melanie's salon and my heart gave a little flutter. I wanted to see my wedding dress again so bad. Did I just call it *my* dress? Oh man, I had it bad. Before I could even go there, I had some questions to ask Gwen.

Gwen was at the front desk, wrapping up some business with a client.

"Can I help you with something?" Another consultant asked me. I recognized her from last night's vigil.

"No, I'm just waiting for Gwen." At the sound of her name, Gwen turned her attention my way and gave a little wave. While she was finishing up, I set my sights on the shoe display. A pair of high-heeled, open-toed beauties caught my eye. With those babies, I might be a full five feet tall. Not to mention they were a perfect match for the dress. I was envisioning the complete look when Gwen walked over to me.

"Aren't those shoes amazing?" she asked.

"They are. I might have to snag them on my way out," and try to keep Finn from seeing them. I wanted my entire look to be a surprise.

"I'll have Kelly grab your size if you want to try them on."

"I would love to, but first, I was wondering if you had a minute to chat." I leaned in closer. "About Melanie."

Gwen nodded. "We can chat in my office."

I followed Gwen to the back behind the reception area and down the hall to her office. It was straight across the hall from Melanie's. I would've loved to peek in and see if the gorgeous gown was still hanging on the back of her door, but unfortunately, it was closed.

"Come on in," Gwen said. I took a look around. Whereas Melanie's office had been full of binders, catalogs, and calendars, Gwen's office was a designer's workshop. The entire sidewall had been upholstered with a tufted gray fabric. Strands of pearls, lace, and fabric swatches of various textures, all in shades of white and cream, along with a dozen or so sketches, were pinned to it. Across from her desk sat a round table with stacked sketchbooks, pencils, pins, and a measuring tape. Just looking around inspired me. I hadn't previously thought of it, but I was going to ask Finn about adding a designated workstation to our houseboat. The renovations were slow going, seeing as Finn spent most of his time on the water, but the improvements he had made were just how he had pitched it.

I stopped daydreaming and sat down across from Gwen, who was seated behind her glass-topped desk.

"How's the store doing?" I asked.

"It's chaos, but we're figuring it out as we go. The team has some ideas on how we can stay open and still honor Melanie's work."

"I'd love to hear more about that."

"It's in the early stages, but we have enough stock and Melanie's designs to last us through the next year. After that?" Gwen shrugged her right shoulder. "We're thinking about trying to continue Melanie's style through our own designs. We all shared a common vision with Melanie, so we feel it should be something we can pull off. Hopefully. We thought of changing the store name to something along the lines of Bridal inspired by Melanie May, too. Not sure yet."

"That sounds like a great idea," I said.

"It's really the only one we've come up with. I'd rather not even have to think about it, but I would also hate to see all of Melanie's hard work in creating this brand and company disappear."

"When you're ready, let me know. I can probably help with the branding. In fact, that's what I just presented on this morning at the women's leadership conference. Let me know if that's something you're interested in."

"That would be wonderful. I'll keep that in mind. Now what can I do for you?"

"Well, I've picked up little bits and pieces about Melanie's life from those who were close to her, like yourself. One of the things I've heard is that Melanie and her mom didn't get along. I would've never guessed that from talking with her, though."

Gwen rolled her eyes. "Of course not. I'm sure Veronica was all about herself. Poor me. Poor Melanie. Why did this happen to her?"

"Wow, that's impressive and pretty much spot on."

"I've watched Melanie deal with her mom for years. To say they didn't get along, well, that's an understatement. Melanie tried, and I honestly feel that she deeply loved her mother, but it was one-sided. The only person Veronica loves is herself."

"Would you say she was jealous of her daughter?"

"Absolutely. No question about it. Veronica always wanted the success that Melanie naturally achieved. I swear, she would go out of her way to hurt Melanie. Like publicly degrading her work or insulting her love life. You know that voice in the back of your head? The one that causes you to question yourself? Yeah, Melanie had one, a loud one, by the name of Veronica Mays."

"Sounds like the woman has issues."

"Big ones."

"Do you know anything about the lawsuit between Melanie and Veronica?"

Gwen cocked her head. "Lawsuit? No, Melanie never said anything of the sort."

"Do you by chance know where Melanie got the money to open the store?"

"No, not fully. Money was the only thing that we didn't talk about. I know she had some interest from investors and she did receive a business grant from the city, but I never asked for the dollar figures."

"Okay." I tried to hide the disappointment in my voice. I was hoping Gwen would know more details.

"Sorry. I wasn't involved in any part of that side of the business. Design? Yes. Money? No. The thought of bookkeeping freaks me out, but I guess I better get over it if we're going to keep the salon open."

I tried to think of the best way to frame my next question. "Given what you've said, and based on what else I've heard, any chance Veronica would kill her daughter?"

Gwen looked conflicted. "I would love to say no. The thought of that seems so horrific that I don't want to even fathom it, but then I think about how selfish and greedy Veronica could be. If money was involved and somehow Veronica could benefit from Melanie's death, then I have to admit it's a possibility. As much as it sickens me to."

"I'm sorry, Gwen. We'll figure this all out. I promise."

"Thanks, Ziva. How about we lighten the mood?" Gwen pushed off from her desk and stood up. "Do you want to try on those shoes?"

"Oh, that reminds me. There's something else I want to talk to you about. The dress." This got Gwen's attention. "I was wondering if we could make a deal. That is, if you could refund Lucia her money and make the dress available for purchase again?"

"What do you have in mind?"

"I had the idea during my morning branding presentation when someone asked me if I had any new products in the works. I'm just brainstorming here, but what if I created a bridal skincare line and gave your salon exclusive rights for the first quarter in exchange for the dress. Would you be interested in something like that?"

"I'd have to run it by the team, but I'm definitely interested."

"I'd be happy to show you guys some estimated figures based on my past product launch. It would give you an idea of what type of revenue you would be looking at. It could easily be $100,000."

"With numbers like that, we wouldn't dare say no. If the figures are as high as you say they are, you can consider it a deal."

"Excellent. I'll have those figures sent over along with the preliminary contract for you guys to take a look at. Sound good?"

"Definitely. I'll get the team together and we'll discuss it as well. I'll also look into refunding Lucia's credit card."

"Great. I'm scheduled to fly out on Wednesday night, but maybe I can meet with you guys before then."

"Okay, let's tentatively plan on Wednesday morning?"

"Sounds good. Now where are those shoes?"

"Do you want to try them on with the dress?"

"I thought you'd never ask."

~

My plan had been to call Detective Hart and tell her what I had heard about Veronica. Then I would call Finn and have him meet me in the lobby and we could set out. Maybe we could do a zip-line adventure or something that he would love.

I dialed Detective Hart's number and was shocked when she answered immediately. "Hart," she said by means of hello.

"Hi, detective. It's Ziva Diaz."

"Ziva, I was just going to call you."

"You were? Have you solved the case?"

Detective Hart ignored my questions. "Tell me, was Lucia dead in her bedroom when you were at her house?"

"What?! No, I swear to you she wasn't. No one was home." No one was home, right? My mind started racing. Had I overlooked something? Was Lucia in her house needing help and I ran the other way? Could the killer have been watching me? I looked suspiciously at the people walking around me.

"Would you be willing to meet me at her house? I'd like to have you confirm a few details."

"I can do that. I'll be there as soon as I can." My hands were shaking when I hung up with the detective. I immediately called Finn.

"Lucia is dead," I said when he answered.

Bless his heart, Finn handled the news better than I had. Must be a relationship hazard. He didn't miss a beat.

"The dress girl?" he asked. I had told Finn about Lucia's twenty-thousand-dollar commissioned dress, leaving out the minor detail that it was also the dress that I had fallen in love with.

"Yep, that's her. Detective Hart is at her house right now. She asked if I could meet her there. I told her I would."

"Where are you now?"

"I just left Melanie's salon. I'll be back to the hotel in a minute. Meet me in the lobby?"

"I'll head down now."

"Thanks, babes."

11

"You and Aria were here once already?" Finn eyed the seedy neighborhood out of the cab's back window. You knew the area was bad if he was nervous. I pointed up the street to where Lucia's house was even though I hadn't needed to. The crime scene van backing out of the driveway was a dead giveaway.

The cab pulled up to the curb, and I tried to offer the driver an extra twenty bucks if he'd hang around for ten minutes and wait for us.

"Not nearly enough, lady," he replied, eyeing the van. Finn paid the regular fare and the man zipped off. We surveyed the house from the road.

There's a certain energy to crime scenes that I've come to expect, from the people going in and out of the house and the EMT on standby to remove the body, to the news reporters and nosey neighbors waiting to get the scoop. That last thought stopped me. I turned to Finn, "Notice anything unusual?"

"Yeah, where is everybody?" he asked.

"Where is anybody," I corrected. The whole scene was way too quiet.

Detective Hart was waiting for us. She stepped off the front porch and met us halfway up the driveway.

"Quiet neighborhood," I said to her when she greeted us.

"Snitches get stitches," she replied.

"What?"

"You don't talk to the cops around here. They don't see us as the good guys."

"Ah, I get it. You keep your mouth shut and you don't get hurt."

"Precisely," she replied.

"Where's the press?" Finn asked.

"Press? They don't cover homicides over here. No one does."

"Lovely," I replied. I reached for Finn's hand. I should've brought chocolate.

"That wasn't there," I said, pointing to the symbol that had been spray-painted on Lucia's front door. The graffiti looked like an upside-down pitch fork with thorns. It gave me chills and it was over ninety degrees out.

"I didn't think so. I figured you would have mentioned it if it had. What about the mess inside? You mind coming with me to take a look?"

Mind? Yes, I did mind, but that's what I was there for. "No, I'm good," I lied. "Lead the way."

Detective Hart made Finn stay outside, which was understandable, but it made me a bit nervous. He looked completely out of place, standing in the middle of the driveway with his hands tucked in his pockets.

Detective Hart must've thought so too. "Why don't you

stand over there close to my car. We'll just be a couple of minutes."

Finn shrugged his shoulders as if to say, "Sure, why not?" and did as was suggested. I felt a pang of guilt. I shouldn't have had him tag along. I should've waited to call him until after meeting Detective Hart.

When we reached the top of the porch steps she turned to me and said, "I'd give my guys hell if they ever did what I'm about to let you do. Understand?"

"Got it."

"Slip these on over your shoes, follow exactly where I walk, and don't touch anything." I did exactly as I was told even though I hated it. Authority figures and I rarely got along. "We've processed the scene, but I want to make sure we're not missing anything. Seeing you were just here, we can sketch a before and after comparison. I'm not going to pass that up."

"Even if it is against protocol?" I'm sorry, but I couldn't help it. If she was going to boss me around, then I was going to remind her that she was breaking the rules.

"That's my judgement call," Detective Hart said, trying to sound stern, but I saw the corner of her mouth turn up in a smile.

She opened the front door and I walked in after her. "Is this how it looked when you were last here?"

My eyes darted around the room, too quick to really catalog anything. I realized that I was waiting for the Boogey Man to jump out at me. Nervous energy, I told myself. Being in the same house with someone who was just murdered will do that to you. I relaxed my shoulders and surveyed the room, slower this time.

What was different and what was the same? I asked myself. I closed my eyes to picture what the room had previously looked like. The same magazines, laundry basket, and high heels were scattered about, in addition to a coffee table that had since been turned on its side.

"That table wasn't like that yesterday." Detective Hart nodded and made note of it.

We systematically walked through the house, me making sure to walk exactly where Detective Hart had as I pointed out the small differences, like the opened cupboard and knocked-over barstool in the kitchen. We walked into the bedroom last.

"This is where her body was found," Detective Hart said, motioning to the bed.

If I hadn't known that a woman had been murdered in there, I never would have been able to tell. The bedding tossed off onto the floor was the only evidence of the potential struggle.

"What was the cause of death?" The lack of blood had me thinking that it wasn't from a knife or gunshot wound.

"Asphyxiation. With what is yet to be determined. The killer took the evidence with him."

Detective Hart was full of surprises. None of the detectives I knew would have answered that question, nor would they have invited me to a crime scene, or willingly accepted my help. I was starting to like Detective Hart.

I stood with my back to the window and surveyed the room. "Those weren't open," I motioned to the closet doors across from the foot of the bed. Shoeboxes and papers littered the floor.

"What about the dresser?"

"It was like that," I said, referencing the opened drawers. "But there was also a half-packed suitcase on the bed, along with a bunch of clothes and toiletries." I didn't see any of that anymore. "Did she have a car?" I wondered if that's where the suitcase had disappeared to.

"We're looking into it. There's not one in the garage."

I looked hard around the room, trying to spot if anything else was out of place. "Nothing else jumps out at me. I did only get to see the room from the window, so I might be missing something."

"No, that's good." Detective Hart was writing down some additional notes. "Why don't we wrap up this conversation outside."

"I'm not sure how much help I was. Hopefully a little bit. My best guess is that she was ambushed when she came back home to get something," I said as we walked out of the house.

"You're probably right," Detective Hart said.

"So, what, she was killed by a gang?" I pointed to the symbol on the front door.

"Don't know yet. I'm told by my gang unit that this symbol stands for retaliation. Either she was murdered in retaliation or the gang marked the door to let the killer know that her murder won't go unpunished."

Awesome. Gangs were pretty much where I drew the line. Hopefully Lucia's murder had nothing to do with Melanie's. I turned my attention to finding Finn but came up empty. I started to have a mini panic attack when I couldn't spot him. I whipped my head around looking for the guy.

"Where in the devil did he go?" I asked no one in particular.

Detective Hart caught on and started looking also. "Oh no," she said.

"Don't 'oh no' me. If my fiancé's been kidnapped by

some cracked-out gang member, you're going to be in big trouble."

Just then, Finn whistled and caught our attention. I turned and spotted him sitting on the neighbor's front porch with the older man who had scared the crap out of me yesterday.

I gave Finn the same look I imagined a mother giving a child who wandered too far off. Finn waved, seeming amused, with a can of Coke in his hand. Honestly, I shouldn't be surprised. Finn could make friends with a mailbox.

"You might want to check in with the neighbor next door, too. He's the one who told me she had hit the road for Mexico."

Detective Hart nodded. "She was running."

"Any idea why?"

"We're working on it. I started looking into her after you called yesterday. We know she called off her wedding to Federico Metiva. He's high up in the Viper Nation, a particularly violent gang in the area."

"That's why she didn't need the dress anymore and probably how she could've afforded it in the first place," I said.

"Most likely."

"And why she really needed Melanie to refund the cash if she was planning on running." I imagined Lucia having a revelation and trying to escape her life, but it caught up to her instead. "That would also explain why a gang member would kill her and the symbol on the door," I said, continuing my reasoning.

"It would. Disrespect is all it takes," Detective Hart said. I nodded, trying to process it all. "Here, I want to show you something. Maybe it means something to you."

Detective Hart took out her cell phone. I was hoping she was going to have me read a note they found or some other clue, not pull up a picture of Lucia's dead body. I had seen my fair share of dead bodies, but I still didn't want to get all up close and personal with them. Detective Hart zoomed in on Lucia's neck. An intricate pattern was clearly embossed on it. "Anything in the house come to mind that could create this?"

"No, nothing in the house or anything else I can remotely think of, sorry." I shook my head, partially because I didn't know the answer and also to clear the image from my mind.

"It was worth a shot." Detective Hart pocketed her phone.

"Do you think Lucia's and Melanie's murders are related?" I asked.

"Most likely not. So far, the dress is the only thing that connects the two. I can't make any other connection."

"But..." I could sense there was more there.

"I'm not going to completely rule it out. I'm not a fan of coincidences, and this has coincidence written all over it," Detective Hart finished.

That it did.

~

FINN WAS STILL CHATTING with his buddy next door when Detective Hart and I were ready to go. I wasn't up for making small chat, or friends for that matter, so I hollered over to Finn instead.

"Hey, you ready to go?"

"You guys want me to give you a lift?" Detective Hart offered.

"Sure, that would be great," I replied. I had a feeling

we'd be hard pressed to get a cab to come pick us up. Finn jogged back over and I filled him in on Detective Hart's offer. He was quick to accept as well.

"First time in Vegas?" Detective Hart asked as she drove us back to Tourist Town.

"It is," I said, thinking it was going to be the last. I'd had enough of the dry heat, sand, and dead bodies. The warm, salty coastal air and ocean breezes were calling me home. That is, as soon as I solved this case.

"I promise it's much nicer when you don't have to deal with murder," Detective Hart said.

"I imagine it is," I laughed. Finn chuckled for an entirely different reason. Probably having something to do with the fact that I always seemed to find dead bodies.

We had Detective Hart drop us off at the Cosmopolitan, but Finn and I both hesitated walking through the doors.

"What do you want to do now?" I asked him.

"Well, if I know you, I'm betting that you'd like to sit down somewhere to regroup. That, and you're starving."

I hadn't even realized it, but Finn was right.

"I could definitely eat," I said.

"I heard there's an awesome burger joint with the best milkshakes in town," Finn said. I mentally calculated the calories to decide if it was worth it. "They even offer them spiked," Finn added to the temptation. I thought of the way Lucia's dead body had looked. I could definitely use a drink.

"Okay, I'm down. For the record, I'm pretty sure you're what they call an enabler," I told Finn. Like an emotional eater needed any coaxing.

"I am not. I'm starving too and a burger sounds really good. If you want, we could go for a run afterward or just go get a salad."

"Ack, no! I mean, I didn't bring any running shoes and I'm sure we'd be hard pressed to find a salad bar."

Finn laughed at my lame excuses. It was true. I hadn't packed any sneakers and I didn't know where to find a good salad. I did, however, have Gwen holding the perfect pair of high heels along with the gown back at the salon. The look was exactly what I was going for. I had just needed to see it to know it. Speaking of the gown, I liked the way it hugged my curves, but I didn't want it too tight.

"How about we walk to this restaurant of yours?" I offered.

See, I wasn't completely lazy.

Finn agreed, but it was pointless in the workout department seeing it was less than a block away. Oh well, I say it was an A for effort.

The fifties-style diner, with a black-and-white checkered floor and red vinyl booths, looked as clichéd as they came until I looked at the menu. Salted caramel crunch milkshakes, BBQ-crusted burgers with smoked gouda, thick-cut steak fries, and onion rings the size of my palm. Yes, please!

"Where do we go from here?" Finn asked after we placed our order.

"Here's the thing: If we take Lucia out of the equation, we're left with Melanie's mom, the designer Paul Frederick, and maybe even Zane. If Lucia somehow still factors in, then I'm not sure. I really don't like gangs. They scare me."

This got a chuckle out of Finn. "Wait a second, back when you thought Vince was part of the Mafia, that didn't stop you from tracking him down, or when we had a homicidal baker poisoning everyone in town, that didn't make you nervous. Oh, and who can forget about the psychopath in Tampa."

"Yeah, yeah, yeah, but this is different."

"No, I don't doubt it is." Finn was clearly amused.

"What is so funny?" I was getting annoyed.

"I'm just relieved to know that you have some sense of fear in you. I was starting to worry."

"If you're not careful I'll put the fear in you," I threatened Finn with a smile on my face.

The waitress set our food down in front of us and gave me the strangest look when I swatted Finn's hand away from my onion rings.

"I like it when you're feisty," Finn said.

"Oh, I'll show you feisty," I playfully bickered back.

A couple bites into our lunches, and we were back to talking about the case.

"What are you thinking for the motives?" Finn asked.

I couldn't answer. I had taken the longest hit off my milkshake. I was sure I was going to get a brain freeze but it was worth it. The saltiness of the caramel, the creaminess of the ice cream, and the final chocolate crunch? Divine. I was in heaven while Finn waited for an answer. What had he asked? Oh yeah. Motives, that's right.

"Jealousy seems to be the number one motivator for both Veronica and Zane. Plus, Veronica has the mindset that she gave up everything for Melanie. I get the sense that Melanie didn't acknowledge that and I don't blame her."

"I don't either. What, she's supposed to apologize for being born?" Finn asked.

"Exactly. It's not her fault that her mother had her priorities in the wrong place."

"Why was Zane jealous?" Finn asked.

"Because Melanie's career took off while his stalled. At least that's one theory. They also had a history of domestic disputes, but I don't know the details. You know what? I can't believe I hadn't thought of it before, but I should give

Cee Cee Thomas a call." She was my reporter friend who worked for Entertainment Now. She had helped me solve the last case with her Hollywood insider knowledge. I would've called her right that second, but that darn milkshake was so delicious.

"What's the story with the designer guy?" Finn asked between bites of his burger.

"Paul Frederick. Long story short, he couldn't stand being upstaged by a new designer."

"He was used to being on top."

"Exactly. His ego took a big hit and from what I hear, he likes to start drama. Must be from getting his start in theater," I joked.

"Have you talked to him?"

"No. He's taken a creative sabbatical." Finn raised his eyebrows. "I know, sounds fishy, right?" I sucked down the last bit of sweet and chocolatey goodness, and then pulled my cell phone out of my purse and made that call to Cee Cee. She didn't answer, but I left her a voicemail.

"Hey, Cee Cee, it's Ziva. You won't believe it, but I'm wrapped up in this Melanie May case. Give me a call when you get a sec. Thanks, girl." I hit end on my cell phone and thought for a minute. "You know, we're not getting anywhere with Zane right this second, but I feel like there's more we can do on the Paul Frederick front. It shouldn't be too hard to track down where he lives. What do you think?"

"I say that's where we should head next," Finn said.

"Have I told you lately how much I love you?"

"I thought you were going to put some fear in me."

"If you're lucky. Now let's finish up lunch and hunt down a designer."

12

We weren't going to be able to just sneak in and snoop around Paul Frederick's condo. He lived in a gated community with security guards who looked like they actually took their job seriously. I eyed the yellow handles of their Taser guns. Yeah, I did not want to experience *that* again. Finn turned around at the next light and pulled over, parking the Mercedes in front of a big-box superstore. Finn and I had borrowed the car from Aria since she and Vince were having a spa day. By borrowed I mean I stopped by Aria's hotel room and whispered to her what we were up to and had her discreetly hand me the keys. It was easier than trying to explain it all to Vince.

"We need a plan," Finn said.

I watched the people walk in and out of the store. "This is going to sound clichéd, but what if I do the whole housekeeper routine?"

"Does this mean you're going to buy a cute little skirt and feather duster? Please say yes."

"Noooo, I was thinking more along the line of a bucket, some bleach, and a roll of paper towels."

"Okay, but for the record, anytime you want to play dress up, I'm down."

"I'll keep that in mind."

We ran into the store and loaded up on some cleaning supplies. I even switched up my wardrobe. To Finn's disappointment, it did not include a cute little skirt, but rather khakis, a white cotton polo shirt, and matching white sneakers. It was the least sexy outfit ever.

"Do you think they're going to believe a housekeeper drives a Mercedes?"

"Maybe I'm a housekeeper with benefits. This is Vegas after all." Finn eyed me. "Do you have a better plan?" I asked not expecting an answer.

Finn thought for a second. "Wait, yes, yes I do. I just can't remember if the sign said it was today or not."

"What sign? What are you talking about?"

"Hang on. Let's do another quick drive-by."

Finn slowed as we pulled up to the entrance and I saw what he was talking about.

"Bingo. An open house. Let's use that as our cover and we can save the housekeeper routine for once we're inside if we need to," he said.

"You're right. That's smarter. Let's do that." I looked down at the clock. The open house was scheduled to run for another 30 minutes. Plenty of time.

Finn drove up to the security stand and rolled down his window. "Hi, we were just driving by and saw the sign for the open house. Is the agent still available?"

"Let me check, sir" The security guard radioed ahead to confirm that the real estate agent was still on the property. "Yes, she's still available. She says she'll meet you at the unit now. Just drive forward here to the stop sign and take a right.

Go down and take a left on Joshua Tree. It's the third condo on the left."

"Great, thanks man. I appreciate it." The security gate lifted up and we drove through.

"Are we really hitting the open house?" I asked.

"Don't you think we should? I don't want to not show up and have security start searching for us."

"Good point. Let's do this whole open house thing and then pretend to drive around looking at the rest of the complex."

"Good thinking."

We turned onto Joshua Tree and counted off the condos. The real estate signs and blue balloons set the townhouse apart from the rest on the street.

"They all look identical. I can't believe Mr. Frederick lives here. It's so vanilla," I said to Finn.

"I take it he's a character."

"When I just Googled him, the first image that came up was him dressed like Willy Wonka. Remember that purple suit?"

"That colorful, huh?"

"You should see his wedding dresses."

We pulled into the driveway and saw the real estate agent waiting to greet us on the adobe-styled porch.

"Hi, you two. My name is Penny Sweets. I'm the real estate coordinator here at Oasis. I'm so happy you were able to find us today." And she seriously was. Penny's smile was as bright as the summer suit she was wearing. "Aren't you two just the cutest couple. I bet you hear that all the time."

"Oh, thanks so much," I replied. Maybe this wouldn't be so bad after all.

"Here, come inside out of this heat and I'll give you the full tour."

For as much beige and brown that was in the landscape, you'd think the townhouse's interior designer would've chosen a different color palette to work with. I could've really used an ocean view right about then. But besides all the earth tones, the home was really quite lovely.

"I heard there's a lot of celebrities that live out in Vegas. Do any of them live here?" I asked as we wound up the tour.

"We have our fair share of characters that call Oasis home. I wouldn't say any A-listers, but we have a great community of artists and musicians."

"Artists? Any painters or designers?" I asked.

"Both. The fabulous designer Paul Frederick lives here, as does the painter Ann Marie."

"Did you hear that, honey? We could be neighbors of Paul Frederick. I love his gowns," I said to Penny.

"He does have a certain style about him. In fact, he insists that his front door be painted peacock blue even though it goes against the homeowner's ordinance. He says he doesn't care and pays the fine every month." Penny shrugged her shoulders. "What are you going to do about it?"

We struck gold. This was just the little nugget of information we needed to find his house.

"As for the musicians who live here, it's not unusual to have an impromptu concert by the pool. And speaking of pools, let's ride over there now. You'll be amazed."

The three connected pools and two hot tubs were pretty fabulous. Add in the palm trees, nearby bar, and lounge chairs, and I would consider it a vacation destination. Even with several residents hanging around, the area had plenty of room. The backyard of condos lined one edge of the pool and the one with the peacock blue door immediately caught my eye. Paul Frederick's door was straight ahead. I motioned to Finn. He saw the door too. Maybe I could sneak in through a back entrance? Then I had another thought. I wouldn't need to sneak in if I was his housekeeper.

Meanwhile Penny kept talking about the perks of living at Oasis, "We have a state-of-the-art fitness center if you would like to see that too?" she said.

Only when she stopped and waited for our response did I really pay attention. "Oh, sorry. I was still looking at the pools. They really are amazing," I said, pointing to the waterfall area.

"You have a beautiful ring. Is that a pink diamond?" Penny asked.

"It is."

"I love colored diamonds. I've always wanted a canary. Someday maybe I'll treat myself."

That got a genuine smile out of me. I liked that she was willing to shell out the cash and wasn't sitting around waiting for a man. Naturally, I then felt guilty sitting here wasting her time. She wasn't going to get any commission out of us.

"Thank you so much for all of your time this afternoon. I think the two of us need to chat for a bit and then we'll be in touch. Is that okay with you?" I didn't want to ditch Penny, but wrapping our appointment up was the right thing to do. After she provided her contact information and listed off a few more benefits, Finn and I were on our way, sort of.

"What do you want to do?" Finn asked as he looped around the complex.

"I'm hoping we'll get lucky and I can get in through the back door," I said.

"You?"

"Yes, me. Let me change into my housekeeper digs and then I can pretend to wash the back windows and hopefully find a way in." Truthfully it wasn't the best plan, but it was all I had at the moment.

I slipped into the backseat, shimmied out of my business attire and wiggled into the khakis and button-up shirt. "Let's act like we belong here. How about you switch me spots and I'll park right in the driveway. You hide out in the backseat and call me if anything's up."

"Okay, I can do that."

That's exactly what we did. I parked in the driveway, popped the trunk, took out my cleaning supplies, and walked around to the backyard. A nice family leaving the pool was gracious enough to hold the pool gate open for me as they walked out. Other than them, no one paid any attention to me.

I walked right over to Mr. Frederick's patio door and got to work; housework that is. I sprayed the window down with cleaner and started wiping it clean. Clarissa had said Mr. Frederick was on a creative sabbatical, but I wanted to make sure he wasn't sitting in his living room or something crazy like that. Also, on the off chance that someone was watching me, I wanted to look legit.

Looking in through the window, I could see the house was as clean as could be. There wasn't any food left out, dirty dishes, clothes, nothing. Basically, the exact opposite of Lucia's. I held my breath and took a chance with the sliding patio door.

It was locked.

Crud.

I waited there a second, debating what else I could do. So far, I had only been able to confirm that Mr. Frederick wasn't home. I hadn't seen the man approach me from behind.

"You locked out?" The maintenance worker asked me.

I jumped.

"Sorry, I didn't mean to scare you. I just saw you try the door."

"Oh, yes, I can't believe it. I keep forgetting Mr. Frederick's door's lock after themselves. He's going to think I'm an idiot." I took my phone out and pretended like I was looking for his contact information. "I hope he doesn't fire me," I added.

"Listen, I'm not supposed to do this, but I don't want you to get fired. I can run to the office and get his spare and let you in, just this once."

"You would do that for me? You would be really helping me out." I said.

"Yeah, I guess I can. Just don't tell anyone. I don't want to get in trouble either."

"Trust me, I won't. Promise." I said.

"Just give me a couple of minutes and I'll be right back."

As soon as the maintenance guy took off, I texted Finn. *Maintenance guy letting me in. Be out front in a minute.*

It took the guy less than three minutes to come back with the key. He met me on the front porch and undid the lock.

"Nice car, by the way," he said.

"Thanks. It's my dad's." The guy nodded and I hoped that explained how I could afford such a luxury.

"Maybe I'll see you around sometime?" he asked.

"Yeah, maybe. Thanks again for saving my tail," I said.

"You're welcome. The job market out here is brutal."

I laughed. "That it is. I better get back to it, then," I said, walking in and pretending I knew where I was going, but at that moment, I had a horrifying thought: I sure as sugar hoped Mr. Frederick lived alone. Not my best thought-out plan ever. No one came running downstairs and I didn't hear any voices or televisions. The only thing I could hear was the faint sound of water running, like a fountain or a fish tank low on water. Hopefully this meant that I was in the clear. I trod lightly through the foyer anyway.

The first thing I spotted was a set of crystal food bowls on the ground in the kitchen. A lace doily was placed underneath them. Talk about fancy pet bowls. A purple silk pillow with gold tassels and the name Queenie embroidered on it was adjacent. My first thought was Mr. Frederick owned a cat; that is, until I saw the gold-framed, wall-size print of a French bulldog in the living room. An ivory plush pillow was in this room as well, with a basket of toys and an-honest-to-goodness treat station for the pup. Some people had coffee bars, Frederick had a puppy refreshment station. I kid you not. That's what the sign said. The area was even equipped with a self-dispensing treat toy and pink-porcelain water fountain. That's the tinkling sound I heard. By these standards, Captain Jack was neglected.

Focus, I told myself. I needed a clue as to where Mr. Frederick had escaped. Walking into every room was like looking through a kaleidoscope, an explosion of colors. At this rate, a piece of white paper like a travel itinerary would stick out like a penguin standing on a snow bank.

I went upstairs and looked in the master bedroom. It looked like a circus. I'm serious. A plush red and white stripped comforter was on the end and an enormous stuffed elephant stood in the corner. The faint smell of popcorn lingered in the air. The room was eclectic, but it was also spotless. I moved on.

I suppose the next room would be considered the office, except it lacked traditional office furniture. Everything was inflatable. The couch, chair, table. The neon blow-up furniture was different to stay the least. The only thing more bizarre was the patterned-fabric-covered walls. The room was totally trippy. All that was missing were a couple blacklights.

I was about to write the room off when I noticed the closet door was open. Inside, set up on a set of built-ins, was an old-school desktop computer. If I was lucky, it wouldn't ask for a password. If I was really lucky, he hadn't cleared his browser history. I started the computer and was about to walk over to the window to look out for Finn when a brick came crashing through the window.

I jumped back, turning my face away from the explosion of glass. And that's when the Molotov cocktail flew past me, bouncing off the blowup couch and hurling itself back toward me. I ducked. The glass shattered above my head, sending flames and fuel across the walls.

The problem with a room covered in fabric is that it goes up in flames like a dried-out lighted Christmas tree with faulty wiring. The only thing more intense than the heat was the smoke. The room was engulfed in it. I army crawled to the hallway. Instinctively my eyes were closed. I debated if I should turn right or left, trying to remember which was the way back downstairs when I heard Finn calling my name. Screaming was more like it.

"ZIVA! ZIVA!" I couldn't respond. My heart was hammering and I felt like my lungs were filled with smoke. But the sound of Finn's voice was all I needed to know which way to go. I found my courage, jumped to my feet, and started racing down the hall, running right into my man. Hand in hand, we raced out of the condo and jumped into the Mercedes.

"Sweet sugar!" I said to Finn, gasping for air and trying to catch my breath. Finn chose a different expletive. His was more in line with how I felt, but not suitable to type.

"You're bleeding." Finn turned my cheek ever so closely toward him. Now that he mentioned it, it did sting. I put the visor down and flipped open the mirror to see for myself. My face was speckled with tiny cuts, nothing too deep, but we'd have to make sure to get the glass out.

I clicked on my seatbelt, "Just drive, we'll figure out the rest." Firetrucks, an ambulance, and police cars were already pouring into the complex when we turned out.

13

"Slow down," I said to Finn. He was pushing sixty miles per hour, and I wasn't about to escape a firebombed apartment just to get pulled over by the police for speeding and end up being questioned anyway.

"I'm okay." I reached over and put my hand on Finn's thigh and gave it a little squeeze. Finn looked at me and I saw the anger there, smoldering inside. I took my hand off his leg and shifted my gaze out the window.

"Sorry, it's not you. It's not you," Finn said. I wasn't sure I believed him. "I'm serious. It's the rest of the world I have a problem with. The ones that seem bent on maiming you."

"Did you see the person?" I asked.

"No, I didn't even get the make of the silver car. I ducked when they slowed down in front of the townhouse. I didn't even realize what they'd thrown until I saw the smoke."

"I've royally messed up my Karma," I said.

"I don't know about that. You're a good person. Your heart's in the right place."

"You think I should give up?" I wasn't sure I would be able to, but I would try if that's what Finn wanted.

"I'm not saying that. It's just, I'm sick of feeling like I'm going to lose you. This week has been crazy. You've stopped my heart more than once and I think I'm going to need a pacemaker after all of this." He said the last part with a smile, but I knew what he meant. I was a smart woman who was making stupid moves lately. Either that or I needed to reevaluate my hobbies. It was probably a combination of both.

"I shouldn't have let you go in there—"

"Come on, that's ridiculous. You know very well that I wouldn't get me a second look walking into that townhouse, but you probably would've gotten reported in a heartbeat. A Latina-looking woman with a bucket and cleaning supplies never gets noticed. It was a smart plan." Well, smart enough. I hadn't shared with Finn my second thoughts I had about a roommate after I entered the house.

"Not that any information you found would be worth it, but did you find anything?"

"I wish I could say—" I stopped myself and thought about Frederick's French bulldog. "Wait just a second, I might have. Let me make a quick phone call. In the meantime, head to a pharmacy. With some tweezers, peroxide, and first aid cream, I should be good to go. Oh, and don't forget the chocolate. Lots of it. And maybe some gin," because I could sure use a dirty martini.

"Hey, Clarissa. Ziva. You haven't by chance heard from Mr. Frederick, have you?"

"Actually, I did today." I let out a relieved breath. It was good to know that he was still alive.

"He didn't tell you where he was staying at, did he?"

"He didn't, and honestly I didn't even think to ask. Why?"

Here's where things got a little tricky. I wanted a solid

reason as to why I was asking without making Clarissa suspicious. I went with a half-truth. "I was just visiting a friend who lives by him when we heard there was a fire. I guess a pretty big one. I just wanted to make sure his puppy wasn't home."

"Oh my gosh, that's awful. No, Queenie is probably with Ms. Darla. Mr. Frederick trusts only her with his little precious pooch."

"Ms. Darla?"

"Darla Reynolds. She owns Puppy Dreams, the dog resort in town."

"Awesome. I'll give her a call. Maybe she can let him know. Also, if you talk to him again, can you give him my number?"

"Yeah, sure. No problem."

"Thanks, Clarissa!"

WHILE FINN GOT the medical supplies, I did a little research before making my next call. My first idea was to pretend to be the office manager at Oasis trying to get a hold of Mr. Frederick due to the fire, but I thought that might be a bit of a stretch. How would the office manager know to call Puppy Dreams? I also didn't want Ms. Darla to offer to pass the message on. No, I needed a more personal reason for requesting the information. I didn't know how well Ms. Darla knew Mr. Frederick's family. Hopefully it wasn't well, but I couldn't take any chances.

"Puppy Dreams," a woman said into the phone.

"Hi, is this Miss Darla?" I asked as Finn got back in the car.

"Why yes dear, what can I do for you?"

"My name is Taylor Ray. I'm Mr. Frederick's niece." Thanks to Google, I knew that Mr. Frederick did in fact have a niece named Taylor. She was his sister's daughter and an aerialist. According to the fashion columns, the two collaborated on costumes for her performances. "We've had a family emergency with my mom and I can't get a hold of my uncle. He isn't answering his cell phone. You don't by chance know where he's at do you?"

I could tell that Ms. Darla was debating giving up any information.

"He told me that you would have Queenie. I'm sure he told you where he was staying. I would ask my mom, but well, she's not conscious." Finn was looking at me wide-eyed, like he couldn't believe the lies that were coming out of my mouth. I looked at him and mouthed, *What?* He shook his head.

"Did he provide a number where he was staying? It's really important. My poor mom. My uncle would be devastated if she should pass without a chance for him to say goodbye," I added.

That last part did the trick. "Yes, yes, yes. He did. I'm so sorry to hear about this, sweetie. I have the resort information written down right here. Just give me a minute and I'll go get it." I gave Finn a thumbs-up.

"Okay, here it is." I scrambled to come up with something to write with. A tube of lipstick and the back of my checkbook would have to work. "He's staying at Crystal Bay Resort in Belize. Here's the number."

I wrote down the digits she read off. "Awesome. Thank you so much. I knew if anyone could help us it would be you. You're an angel." After a few more thank-yous and you toos, I hung up the phone and found Finn staring at me in disbelief, again.

"Stop looking at me like that!" I said to him.

"That was quite the performance."

"Did you want me to get the information or not? I mean, didn't someone just try to burn me to a crisp? I don't know about you, but I want some answers."

"Uh yeah, um, right. I do too."

"Okay then. Let's go to Belize," I said.

"Wait, what? We can't just run off to Central America."

"What else do you suggest we do?"

"Call the number and speak to the man," Finn suggested.

"What am I supposed to say? 'Hi, you don't know me, but I was just snooping around your home office and it was firebombed. We need to talk.'" It seemed impossible to explain any of this via a phone call. Especially to a person I had never met before.

"Okay, call Detective Hart then. You don't have to tell her about the firebomb, but you can tell her you know where Mr. Frederick is staying. I'm sure she can track him down through the proper channels."

I folded my arms across my chest. Finn's suggestion was more rational and responsible, if not also anticlimactic. "Fine, I'll let Detective Hart know, but if anyone else tries to kill me, we're going to Belize."

"Deal. And look, I got the gin." Finn held up a bottle of top shelf.

"Forget the gin. Right now, I need another one of those delicious shakes."

14

Finn and I spent the night in and no one could fault us for that. Even relaxing in the hotel room, my mind continued to race. What did the numbers and notecards in Melanie's desk mean? Who wanted to kill Mr. Frederick? Was it the same person who had killed Melanie and/or Lucia? Was Veronica somehow involved? This case really had me stumped.

On top of all that, Melanie's presentation was being replaced by a roundtable of guest speakers. It was a last-minute scramble, and I told the conference organizers that I would help. I figured it was the least I could do, seeing as I pretty much blew off the rest of the scheduled events. This is also why I agreed to attend tonight's networking event at Studio One, the art gallery downtown. Obviously, all of this was before a firebomb was chucked at my head yesterday. I couldn't back out now, which meant I had to be back at the conference hall by 10 AM. Sigh.

I put on a pair of white slim-legged pants, a flowy peach shirt, and nude peep-toe heels. It was as much energy as I was willing to spend. I didn't care if we were in Vegas or not. That was as glammed up as I was getting.

I was going to grab a quick bite downstairs when Aria texted me.

Got a minute for breakfast?

I looked at the clock. It was just after 9AM. *If we stay on site. Have to be at conference at 10AM.* Aria was good with that. I left Finn to sleep in and met Aria downstairs at Morning Euphoria. The local hot spot was famous for its upscale breakfast spread.

"How was your spa day?" I asked when Aria joined me at the table.

"Good," Aria said, staring at my face. My expert Beauty Secrets makeup skills weren't enough to fool her critical eye. I knew she was dying to ask me about it, but our waiter stopped by at that minute.

"I'll start with some orange juice," I said.

"The same," Aria said. "With vodka," she added under her breath.

The waiter nodded and walked away.

"What in the world happened to you?!" Aria practically shrieked once we were alone.

"Firebomb at Paul Frederick's apartment." I ignored Aria's horror-struck expression and grabbed a slice of banana bread from the basket on the table. "See, aren't you glad I took Finn with me instead? I bet the spa was much nicer."

Speaking of spa days, maybe I would book one tomorrow. Surely, I deserved one. Wait, didn't I have a meeting with the Senses spa manager tomorrow to talk product placement? I'd have to check my email to see if she confirmed.

While I mentally reviewed my schedule, Aria's expression thawed and out tumbled a stream of questions. "The police, did you call them? Do you know who did it or why? Did they get caught?"

"No to all of the above. I'm still trying to piece a few things together myself before I call anyone. Although I promised Finn I would tell Detective Hart and not fly off to Belize."

"Belize?"

"That's where Mr. Frederick ran off to."

"You don't know why someone would firebomb his townhouse?" Aria asked.

"Not really. The only two theories I have is that either someone wanted to kill him, or possibly destroy evidence. The Mercedes was parked in his driveway, so if someone was watching the house, maybe they saw the car there and thought that meant he was back in town. As for the evidence, I'm not sure what it could be. I didn't get a chance to find anything significant." My train of thought stopped there. Sitting a few tables behind us and looking fabulous was Veronica Mays and she wasn't alone. A gentleman in business attire sat across from her. I could only see his side profile, but it wasn't anyone I recognized.

"Look who's over there," I said.

Aria did a double take. "She's looking pretty good," Aria replied.

"Compared to how I left her last night? You could say that again." Her blonde hair was perfectly styled. Her nails painted red. The white collar of her blouse was open enough to reveal a beautiful turquoise necklace. A matching ring sat prominently on her middle finger.

"What's your take, business or pleasure?" I asked.

Aria studied them before responding. "I'm going to go

with business. They're both staying in their own personal space. Look at how her hands are folded in front of her."

"This must be why she couldn't meet with me this morning. It must be important. Wonder if it has anything to do with Melanie."

"What does Veronica do?" Aria asked.

"Like for a living? She's a ballet dancer," but as I said the words, that answer sounded completely ridiculous. "Come to think of it, that doesn't make any sense." How could a semi-retired, single ballet dancer afford the lifestyle Veronica lived? "Wonder where her money comes from."

Aria and I watched Veronica take a legal-size envelope out of her bag and hand it to the gentleman. Our eyebrows rose.

"Maybe the secret is inside that envelope," Aria said.

I wondered what could be inside. Money? Documents? "Maybe he's her lawyer and they're meeting about Melanie's estate," I said.

"That would make sense," Aria said.

I had no idea who Melanie's beneficiary was, but it would make sense that it was her mom since she wasn't married and didn't have any siblings. Then again, if she and her mom really were as estranged as Shelly and Gwen said they were, then anyone could stand to gain her inheritance. The question then became, who benefited from Melanie's death. Zane? I couldn't see how. Mr. Frederick? One less competitor, but that didn't explain why his townhouse was targeted. Veronica? I stared at the woman, sensing there was more than met the eye.

I took out my phone and pretended to take a photo of Aria, but instead snapped a couple pictures of Veronica and the mystery man.

Veronica left shortly after handing the envelope over.

She didn't even stay for a drink. The older gentleman, on the other hand, called the waiter over and proceeded to order. He didn't look to be in a hurry. I casually kept an eye on him while Aria and I ate our breakfasts, but nothing remarkable happened. He had no other visitors and didn't even chat on his phone.

I looked at my phone. It was already 9:45 AM. "I hate to leave you, but I have to head back to the conference. Want to meet up later?"

"Absolutely. Give me a call when you're done and we'll figure out what's up."

"Okay, girlie. I'll see you in a bit."

I HIT the conference floor and was headed to the scheduled room when my cellphone rang. It was Cee Cee.

"Hey, thanks for calling me back. How's it going?" I asked.

"I'm thinking better than you," Cee Cee laughed. "What happened?"

"I was involved in a helicopter crash that landed right by Melanie's body."

"What?!"

"I know, trust me. I can't make this stuff up. Anyway, you know me. I'm working with the police out here trying to piece it together, which leads me to you. I need a favor."

"What's up?"

"Don't laugh, but I need to get an audience with Zane Richards."

It didn't work. Cee Cee laughed anyway.

"Girl, I've been trying to get a statement from Zane since

Friday. No luck. His publicist hasn't returned any requests for comment. I'm not sure I'm going to be much help here."

"I get that, but I thought if you told him I found Melanie's body, he might be willing to talk to me. He might have the missing pieces to the puzzle and not even realize it."

"I can give it try."

"You can also let his publicist know that I've already taken statements from Melanie's mom and her best friend. I'm sure once he hears that, he'll want to set the record straight."

"I saw Veronica's press conference," Cee Cee said.

"Brutal, huh?"

"Glad she wasn't going to be my mother-in-law." I was too. Heck, I didn't even know my future mother-in-law, but then again, Finn didn't know her either.

"I'll try my best. Would you be willing to share what you find out with me?"

I was prepared for this question. Cee Cee was a reporter first. Who could blame her with a story this big? "How about I'll tell you whatever I can that doesn't compromise the case. Is it a deal?"

Cee Cee kept me hanging for a second. It didn't matter how long she kept me waiting. That was the best deal she was going to get and she knew it.

"Okay, deal. I'll call his publicist now."

"Thanks. girl. I owe you."

"You do," she replied.

I hung up with Cee Cee and walked into the conference room. The place was already filling up.

I didn't think I would hear anything back from Zane so soon. I was wrong. Three minutes after I talked to Cee Cee, my phone rang from an unknown number. I took a chance and answered it.

"Hello, this is Ziva."

"Hi, Ziva. Zane Richards." It's one thing to know you gave your number to a rock star, but it's completely another to have them call you directly. I was expecting his publicist to call or some other agent on his behalf. Not the rock icon himself.

Now was not the time to go off and fangirl on the poor guy, but I'm embarrassed to admit it was pretty hard not to. I'm blaming it on his throaty, British voice. I bet he was sitting in his hotel room, wearing tight black jeans and smoking a cigarette. A look that should *not* be sexy, but somehow, he made it so. I shook my head to come back down to Earth.

"Hi, Zane. Thanks for getting back with me. I'm really sorry to hear about Melanie."

"Yeah, it's a right nightmare."

"Um... yeah, I guess it is. Anyway, I'm working to help solve Melanie's murder. I've had a chance to talk to Veronica and Gwen, but I need your piece of the puzzle. Would it be possible for me to ask you a few questions?"

"Probably not a good idea."

"I promise you it's off the record." Sorry, Cee Cee. "I just want to help Melanie."

Zane was silent.

"Listen, I can tell you that what Veronica and Gwen have told me and what I've shared with the police, it doesn't make you look good. Now, maybe you're guilty. If that's the case, turn yourself in. But I'm betting you're not."

"And?"

"I would think you'd want to help catch your fiancée's killer and clear your name. Am I wrong?"

"MGM penthouse. Noon." And the line went dead.

"Okay then," I said to no one. That gave me an hour and a half. Hopefully the roundtable discussion wouldn't drag on.

I was wrong. The discussion did drag on, and on, and on. An hour and fifteen minutes into it, I excused myself from the panel stating a business emergency, and put the conference hall behind me. I needed to think this through. I understood why Zane couldn't meet in a public place and why going to him was easier. I was just going to have to convince Finn of that. I could have easily told him that I had some stuff to do at the conference and ran to meet Zane real quick, but that wasn't the way we rolled. We valued honesty above all else in our relationship. I knew Finn wasn't going to like it, but I was going to meet Zane.

I called Finn. He answered immediately.

"Hey, Zane called me back, but here's the thing. He wants me to meet him at his hotel room."

"Not happening. I'm not comfortable with that."

"I know you're not, but I need to talk to him."

"Ziva, we don't know the guy. Right now, he's a murder suspect."

"And he's going to remain one unless I rule him out."

"I'm coming with you."

"No, you're not."

"Ziva, be smart. What if this guy has nothing left to lose?" Finn had me there.

"Okay, you can come along, but you're not coming into his room. He won't talk to me with you there. I know he won't."

"Fine, but I'm standing outside the door."

"In the lobby," I countered.

"Outside the door, but I'll wait until you go in so he doesn't see me."

I blew my bangs out of my eyes. I should have never cut them. "Fine. Meet me in the lobby now or I'm leaving without you."

15

Walking into the MGM Grand, I couldn't help but feel like someone was watching me. I was probably being paranoid knowing I was going to meet a famous rock star that hundreds of people would love to talk with at that moment. Nervous energy. Yes, that's exactly what it was. I set my shoulders back and stood tall, hoping my confidence would help the nerves dissipate.

"How about you head up and then I'll wait a minute and take the next elevator," Finn offered.

"Okay. I have my cell phone right here." I didn't think I'd need it, but Finn was right, you never knew.

Zane answered the door, wearing tight black jeans and a matching shirt. I knew it! I gave an inward smile. All that was missing was the cigarette. Never mind. I spotted the tendrils of smoke rising from the ashtray on the black baby grand piano framed by the floor-to-ceiling windows. Naturally, the curtains were mostly closed.

Zane looked rough, sporting patchy stumble and dark circles under his eyes. His usual brown spiky hair was flattened forward. He held the door open for me to come in and padded barefoot to the piano. I walked into the room and tried not to stare. The piano was just the beginning. There were couches everywhere. And marble. And I'm pretty sure more than one bathroom. The kind with impressive soaking tubs and vitamin-infused showers and bath tea bags.

I wasn't sure where I should stand. Next to the piano? In front of it? Behind him? I settled on staying off to the side, half-sitting on the arm of the couch, next to the electronic aromatherapy diffuser and dawn simulation remote. So, this was how the rich stayed in Vegas. I would have to let Aria know we were slumming it.

Without saying a word, Zane sat down in front of the piano and started mindlessly playing a song. It started as a lullaby with a slow flowing melody. The softer, higher notes echoed around the room. It was surprisingly beautiful and unlike anything I had ever heard him play before. The song gradually shifted. The tempo increased and the notes turned sharp. Zane's fingers flew across the keys. He started hammering the song out, almost frantically as if he were racing against time. The words "tortured soul" came to mind.

Zane continued to play and the minutes ticked by. I looked at my phone and saw Finn had texted.

Is that a piano?

Yes. He hasn't talked yet.

I had a feeling that this could go on for a while. I didn't have a while. I stood up and walked around in front of Zane. I thought for a minute that maybe he was in concert mode, but then I realized that his eyes were closed, lost in the music. If it wasn't so important for me to talk with him, I would've just walked out and let him be, but that wasn't the case.

My fake cough landed on deaf ears. As did clearing my throat. I would have to do something more direct.

"Excuse me, Mr. Richards?"

Nothing.

I touched Zane on the shoulder.

"What?" he asked, startling as if I had just woken him up.

"Sorry, I don't want to interrupt you, it's just that I have someone waiting for me."

Zane stared at me seeming to think about who I was and why I was standing there. "You're lucky," he finally said.

"Thank you," I replied, not sure if that was the correct response.

Zane eyed me again over the smoke from his cigarette. I could feel the sorrow roll off him in waves. If I stayed in this hotel room much longer, I'd be depressed.

"Listen, I can only imagine how hard this is for you. If I could just ask you a couple of questions and then I'll get out of your hair."

"What is it you want to know?" Zane asked while stamping the cigarette out.

"I saw you at the fight Friday night," I said.

"Bloody criminals. Nobody cares about your feelings when you're an object," Zane replied.

"You were under contract?" I asked.

Zane nodded. "I had to be there or deal with a lawsuit, so Zane The Rock Star showed up."

I thought of something else. "Who was the brunette with you?"

"My sister and date fill-in. I dread the day when she tells me to bug off."

Oh. Well, that wasn't as scandalous as I had thought.

Zane looked at me appearing to wonder if that was the only reason I had interrupted him.

"Can I ask why the silent treatment? Why not release a public statement?" I asked.

"Why should I have to?"

"You shouldn't. But out of respect for Melanie, it would be nice for you publicly acknowledge her passing."

"I didn't think of it that way." Zane lit another cigarette. I felt compelled to open a window and not just for the fresh air. A little more sunlight in the room wouldn't hurt the man either.

"What should I say?" he asked.

"What they always say. Something like: I'm heartbroken to have lost the love of my life. Melanie was an amazing person, my best friend, and she will always be missed. I ask that you respect my privacy during this difficult time. You know, something like that."

"Yes that, what you just said. Have them run that," Zane took a deep drag while I tried to remember exactly what I had just said.

"How about I text the statement to Cee Cee Thomas. You can approve it before I hit send." I already had my cell phone out, shooting off a quick text to Finn to let him know that things were okay and I'd be done in a couple of minutes. Zane nodded that the text would be okay, so that's what we did.

I preempted the statement by texting Cee Cee. "This statement is just for you...and your millions of viewers. You're welcome." After I sent both the message and statement to her, she responded with enough smiley-faced emoticons to let me know she was ecstatic.

"Okay, that's done. Now what can you tell me about Melanie and her mom?" I asked.

Zane responded with a short, four-letter word that described Veronica in a very unfavorable light.

"Got it." No need to take notes on that one. "Is there any truth to Veronica giving Melanie money to start up her business?"

"I doubt it. Where would Veronica get it from? She's a has-been ballerina. Make that a never-has-been."

"Did you by chance lend Melanie the money?" I asked.

"She wouldn't take it. Melanie could be stubborn. Besides, her father beat me to it."

"Her father? I thought she didn't know him?"

"Viktor? Oh, she knows the bloke, all right."

"He's a Russian ballet dancer, right?"

This response got a genuine laugh out of Zane. His eyes lit up and he actually placed his hand on his stomach to stop himself from laughing so hard.

"Viktor can't even walk in a straight line without stumbling over his feet. That is if he could see them."

"So, he's a bigger guy," I said.

"In more ways than one. Viktor is about Viktor and his power and his money."

"What does he do then?" I asked.

"He's a financier. A patron of the arts. A man who hates me."

"You clearly know him then."

Zane stood up, took his cigarette with him and headed to the wet bar to fix himself a drink. I shook my head no when he offered the bottle of whisky to me. Zane balanced the cigarette between his lips and used his pointer finger to stir his drink together.

"Viktor and I didn't agree. He thought I wasn't good enough for Melanie and I thought I was." I waited for Zane to take a drink and let him continue. "Last week when we announced our engagement, Melanie got a call from him. He said that was enough. She needed to end her relationship with me or face the consequences. She gave an exclusive interview to Entertainment Now instead. Then she disappeared."

"Wait, her father threatened her and when she didn't comply she was murdered?"

"I believe so."

Wow. "Where's Viktor now?"

"Probably back in Russia. You're never going to touch him, and I have the rest of my life to blame myself for Melanie's death."

"It's not your—" I started to say.

"Don't say it. It *is* my fault. I should've walked away. I wasn't strong enough." Zane downed his drink.

"Where were you Wednesday night?" I asked. His fiancée was being honored with some big award and Zane was nowhere to be seen.

"Trying to find that strength."

"When's the last time you two talked?" I asked.

Zane seemed to sink down further into despair. "Wednesday afternoon. We'd had a bit of a row after Melanie gave that exclusive interview. I thought it was risky and her father would see it as an insult. Viktor had made it perfectly clear that he wouldn't tolerate open disobedience."

"Out of curiosity, is this what Viktor looks like?" I held my phone out for Zane to see the picture of the man who met with Veronica that morning.

Zane practically growled.

"I take that as a yes." It looked like Viktor was in town. "Listen, don't do anything crazy. Let me take this information to the police. Let them work with it."

Zane didn't answer. I saw him eye the bottle of whisky again.

"I'm going to take off, but here's my number if you think of anything else." I felt like I needed to say something else, like *Don't blame yourself* or *It'll be okay*, but both sounded weak. I ended up with, "The only person at fault here is the one who killed Melanie. Don't forget that."

Zane nodded, but I don't think he was listening.

I left it at that. Finn met me in the hallway.

"How'd that go?" he asked.

"The man's hurting, bad. I don't like him being alone."

"What did he say?"

"Basically, that Melanie knew her father. He's some rich Russian businessman, and he hated Zane. Naturally, Zane believes one hundred percent that Melanie's father is responsible for her death."

"Anything else?"

"Yeah, he doesn't have an alibi for Thursday night."

~

"Where to gumshoe?" Finn asked me when we stepped back onto Las Vegas Boulevard.

"I need to jump online and see what I can find about this Viktor character. I think I'll know more where to go after I do that."

"Do you want to order room service and use your laptop back at the hotel?" Finn suggested.

"Yeah, I think that's an excellent plan."

Two slices of double cheese pizza and a large Coke later and I was finally making some progress.

"Hey babe, look at this."

I was running a title search on Melanie's salon when I

stumbled across my first clue. I turned my screen so Finn could read it. "Viktor's name is listed as the title holder on Melanie's salon. Well Ivankov Trust is; I'm assuming that's him."

"I wonder what other holdings they have?" Finn said.

"Good thinking." I put the trust company's name in the search box and was surprised at the number of results. It looked like Melanie's dad had an impressive portfolio of real estate holdings.

"Look at all these," I said while scrolling through the list. The addresses were scattered all over the country with only two in Las Vegas. One was Melanie's salon and the other one I wasn't sure of. I took an electronic copy of the address and opened another browser window to do a search on it. In less than a second, I had my answer.

"Studio One," I said.

"What's that?" Finn asked.

"It's the art studio where tonight's networking event is set to take place. Melanie had to be involved in setting this up. No way that's a coincidence."

In fact, the coincidences were starting to pile up. In the back of my mind, I had considered blowing off the networking event even though I said I would be there. However, now there was no way I would miss it.

"I need some notecards," I said to Finn. I was already up and looking for my purse. A drugstore was right across the street. I was sure they'd have some.

Finn walked over to the desk and rummaged through one of the shopping bags. Finding what he was looking for, he tossed the pack of cards my way. "I picked some up at the pharmacy yesterday. I knew eventually you would want to lay everything out."

"Thanks babes, good thinking." Did I ever tell you that Finn was a Boy Scout? He was in fact, always prepared.

"I'm going to jump in the shower. I would ask you to join me, but I know your mind's going to be wrapped up in this," Finn said

"That it is, but I'll take a rain check." I was already ripping the cellophane off the cards and looking around for something to write with.

"The pens are in the bag," Finn said as he shucked his shorts and walked off to the bathroom. I had to admit that I did linger on his backside before turning to hunt down those ink pens. The fact that Finn had bought scratch and sniff gel pens just made me love him all the more. Nothing like outlining a murder investigation with adorable novelty pens.

When I was done, I had a chain of events lined across the floor with key characters branching out as needed. We knew that Melanie was last seen when Gwen dropped her off at 1 AM. The last time anyone heard from her was shortly before 1:45 AM. Between that time and us finding her body left about an eighteen-hour window when she was murdered. I was sure Detective Hart had the murder time frame narrowed down more than that.

I then remembered Irene and Eileen, our camping heroes in the desert. I never thought to ask them if they had seen anything suspicious or when they had set up camp. Knowing that information could perhaps narrow down the time frame even further. I jumped up and grabbed my cell phone, hoping I would be able to get a message out to the two ladies. Eileen had said that cell service was spotty, which is why they had the emergency GPS locator. I took a chance and called anyway, leaving them a message when they didn't answer. I knew that they went into town periodically and I could only hope that they would again soon and listen to their messages.

"Hi, guys. It's Ziva. Thanks again so much for being our heroes. I did think of a couple other questions. When you get a chance, could you give me a call back?" I left my phone number and hung up, sitting back to stare at my timeline.

16

Despite my best online search skills, I couldn't find where Viktor lived. However, seeing he had met with Veronica once already that day, I was hoping she could lead us to him.

"How do you feel about doing a little bit of surveillance work this evening?" I popped my head into the bathroom and asked Finn who was just finishing up in the shower.

"That's always a good time. Who's our target?"

"Veronica. Well, technically Viktor, but I'm hoping the two of them meet up again."

"Not a bad plan. Give me ten minutes and I'll be ready to roll," he said.

I called Aria told her I was tracking a new lead and that Finn and I would catch up with her and Vince later. It was hard to make out what she said. From what I gathered, Vince was hitting it big playing craps and the table was a bit rowdy.

Aria stepped away from the table just long enough to offer to call the concierge and have them pull up the Mercedes for us. Finn and I had talked about renting our own car, but accepted Aria's offer once more. Next time I went anywhere on vacation, I was making sure I had my own ride.

"How do you want to do this?" Finn asked me. He was behind the wheel once more.

"Let's do a drive-by first. Veronica's house is about three or four down from a cross-street. I figured we could park on the cross street for a few minutes and keep an eye on her house without being parked directly in front of it." Perhaps we could get lucky and there'd be a nearby house for sale that we could pretend to be interested in.

"This is going to sound goofy, but go to Melanie's salon first. That's the only way I know how to get to Veronica's." I wouldn't say that I was directionally-challenged, but it did take me driving to a place a few times before I could get there via an alternative route.

Finn pulled in front of Melanie's salon so I could take a minute to think the directions through.

"I think I've got it," I said to Finn. I was about to tell him which direction to go when I spotted a woman walking out of the salon. Normally I wouldn't have thought anything of it, except she was carrying Melanie's laptop under her arm.

"That's Melanie's computer," I said.

"What? Are you sure?"

"Positive. The front of her computer has that lotus sticker on it. I saw it when I was in her office Friday night."

"Where is she taking it?" Finn asked as the woman got into her car with the laptop.

"Not only that, but who even is she?" Nothing about her said police. Plus, I was pretty sure the police wouldn't just seize a laptop and put it on the passenger seat of a car. "New plan, follow her. We can track down Veronica after."

So that's what we did, easing into traffic after she did. We didn't have to go very far to get our answer.

"I think I know where she's going." As soon as we turned onto Sunrise Avenue and her car slowed down to turn down the back alley, I was sure of it. "She's going to Studio One. I just saw the address on the title search."

"What do you want to do?" Finn asked.

"Come back tonight. Do you still have a way to contact that buddy of yours?" I asked.

"The hacker?"

"That would be the one. We could use a little bit of help finding out what's on Melanie's laptop."

"Yeah, but I can tell you right now it's going to be trickier. I doubt this girl is accessing Melanie's email. We're probably going to have to manually install the spy tracker software or pay my contact big bucks," Finn said.

"On a scale of one to ten, how illegal is that?" I asked.

"Illegal enough."

"Great. I might be better off calling the police and telling them we saw this girl take Melanie's computer."

"That's not a bad plan either," Finn said.

"I never did call Detective Hart and bring her up to speed. Guess I was hoping to make sense of it all before filling her in." I thought for a moment. "How about we take a step back and go with our original plan of surveying Veronica and see if we can work that angle of the case. Then tonight we can come back to the gallery and I'll see if we can find out who the girl is and why she took the laptop."

"Seems solid."

We did a drive-by past Melanie's salon again, only this time I was able to get oriented and point Finn in the right direction to Veronica's. Fifteen minutes later we were on her street.

"It's right there," I said, motioning to the house directly ahead on the right. Finn slowed down ever so slightly and as he did the garage door started to roll up.

"Eek! Step on it." Finn did just that, zooming past her house, turning the corner, and pulling into the first driveway we saw. I slouched in my seat and watched the top of Veronica's Lincoln drive past while Finn pretended to consult his phone. I didn't even have to tell Finn what to do. A second later he reversed out after her and started tailing the Lincoln.

For the record, it's much easier to tail someone when you're not driving through a neighborhood. I was relieved when she turned onto a busier street and we could hang back a couple of car lengths and still keep a visual. I had no idea where we were going. If it wasn't on the Strip or within a two-mile radius, I was pretty much lost.

Veronica ended up bypassing the Strip, driving through downtown and eventually hopping on I-95. We passed fast food restaurants, doctors' offices, the post office, even the mall, yet Veronica still drove on.

"Where do you think she's headed?" Finn asked me.

"I have absolutely no idea."

I didn't have much time to speculate after that as Veronica finally turned into a strip mall. Finn and I pulled in and kept a safe distance, watching as she parked and walked into a store called Time Again Antiques. Normally I wouldn't find it odd for a woman to go into an antique shop, but I had been inside Veronica's house and her taste was modern all the way. Not only that, but her daughter was murdered a few days ago and now she's, what, going antiquing? That just didn't make any sense.

"What do you think, do we follow?" Finn asked.

"I can't, not unless we want her to see me and I don't

think we do. I do want to see what she's up to in there though."

"Okay, you sit tight. I'm going to run in and see if I can get a read on the situation."

"Okay, but don't get distracted." Antique stores were just older pawnshops and we all know Finn loved his pawnshops.

"Aren't you cute. I'll be right back."

I SWEAR Finn was in the store forever. I was convinced he was going to come back with an armload full of stuff that we'd somehow have to cram into our suitcases for the flight home. I was pretty shocked when he came out empty handed and even before Veronica re-emerged.

"What's the story?" I asked.

'They have a pretty impressive vinyl collection," Finn said with a smile. I gave him *the* look. "She's buying a typewriter."

"What?" I said even though I heard him plain as day.

"She's been heckling over the price for the last twenty minutes. The owner's ringing her up now."

"How much was it?" I asked.

"I think they settled on $800."

"Sweet sugar, are you kidding me? She didn't by chance say what she was using it for, did she?" I asked.

"No, but she was adamant that it had to be manufactured in the 1940s."

I had no idea what to make of this. Maybe she was a collector even though I saw no signs of such a collection in her house and she didn't mention anything about being a writer. Why else would you spend that much money on a typewriter? And why in the world would it matter what year it was manufactured? I thought back to the envelope she had given Viktor that morning. Could the two somehow be related? And if so, what type of documents was Veronica creating? I definitely had more notecards to fill out.

Ten minutes later, Veronica indeed walked out of the shop with a heavy-looking case under her arm. Finn and I watched her pop open her trunk and place the typewriter inside before getting back in her car.

"I'm working on a theory, but I don't have all the pieces. Maybe if I run it by you, you can help me out."

"Shoot," Finn said, pulling back out into traffic a few cars behind Veronica.

"My assumption is that the notecards and numbers in Melanie's desk have something to do with Viktor. He was controlling her business somehow, but Melanie was over it and wanted out. Melanie's intern said she overheard Melanie saying she was tired of caring what other people thought and she was living her life her way now. Plus, Zane said her father told her to break the engagement off and instead she went public with it."

"Okay, I can buy that. Do you think Viktor would kill his daughter over it?"

"I don't know, but if it was as simple as that, then why is someone going after Mr. Frederick? Also, don't forget about Lucia. I can't ignore the feeling that they're all somehow connected, but I can't see how. Why would Viktor kill Lucia? And what could he have against Mr. Frederick?"

"Maybe Viktor saw Mr. Frederick as a threat to the business. Think about it, Mr. Frederick creates this stink about Melanie stealing his designs and suddenly her reputation, and thus Viktor's business, is in the line of fire. I'm betting Viktor went ballistic over it and I don't even know the man."

"That's a good point. I didn't think of that. Okay, so Viktor goes after Mr. Frederick for insulting his daughter's reputation, but then he goes off and murders her? That doesn't add up either."

Finn furrowed his eyebrows in thought. "I feel like we're going around in circles here," he said.

I continued on, "Then you throw in the whole vintage typewriter thing and some random girl driving off with Melanie's computer and nothing makes any sense. I need some chocolate."

Veronica slowed down and turned from the main road into a self-storage unit.

"Keep driving," I said. Even from the road I could see the tall security fence that surrounded the perimeter. Without a keycard or passcode, we wouldn't be able to get through unless we raced and tried pulling in after Veronica and before the gate closed, but I didn't want to take the chance that she'd see us.

"I've got an idea," Finn said.

"What's that?"

"How about we go back to Veronica's and see if she comes home with the typewriter. If not, we know where it's at."

"That's pretty brilliant. We don't have to keep following her around either and run the risk that she sees us."

Thankfully Finn was better with directions than I was and he had us back at Veronica's parked at the opposite cross street and waiting for her to come home.

"There she is," I said after waiting less than ten minutes. The short time frame made it most likely that she hadn't run any other errands. As far as seeing if she brought the typewriter home, we were out of luck. The garage door went up, Veronica drove in, and the garage door went down.

"Well shoot," I said. I looked at the clock, it was almost 4PM. The event at Studio One was scheduled to start at 7PM. "Let's head back and think about how we want to tackle tonight."

~

"Ziva, thank you so much for coming tonight. I wasn't sure if you were still going to be able to make it," Mary, the conference coordinator, said.

"Oh no, I was planning on it. I just had a bit of emergency business to tend to this afternoon," I said.

"Excuse me," Finn said as he touched my elbow and exited the conversation. The plan was for him to get the lay of the land while I worked the room and together we would keep an eye out for the computer girl. At this point I was ready to take the laptop for myself. This was the most frustrating case I'd ever attempted to solve.

I continued to mingle with the conference guests while wait staff made their rounds. Lobster toasts with avocado, spiced warm olives, figs topped with bacon, grilled oysters, caviar tartlets, spinach puffs, and—my favorite—bite-sized red velvet cheesecakes were all presented for us to indulge in. I caught Finn sampling the hors d'oeuvres on more than one occasion. Truthfully, they were pretty darn tasty, especially coupled with the sparkling rosé.

That was it!

No, I hadn't solved the crime, but I did know what to serve our guests at the wedding. From the way Finn was following after the waiter with the lobster toasts, I'm thinking he would agree. Even better was the heavy influence of seafood, which was right up my charter-fishing fiancé's alley.

I caught Finn's eye and smiled as another piece of the wedding puzzle clicked into place. Just then, laptop girl cut across the room and disappeared down the side hallway. Finn nodded, seeing her too, and followed after.

"What did you think about those economic strategies?" A conference attendee asked me.

"Oh, um, yeah, they were brilliant," I said.

"Breaking into the market is such a challenge. I really feel that productivity and sustainability will continue to drive the economy."

I nodded in agreement even though my mind was on Finn. I cased the jointed for about ten minutes before I spotted him again.

"Excuse me, there's someone else I need to speak with," I told the group of ladies. Finn walked across the room in my direction, snagging a glass of rosé for me along the way.

We stood facing a painting of rather menacing-looking clowns and I shuddered, looking at the artist's name in hopes of remembering to never buy their work, but the signature was hard to decipher.

"What did you find out?" I asked him, taking a sip of the pink bubbly.

"There's an office supply room right next to the bathrooms. The girl's walked in and out of it a handful of times. It doesn't appear to be locked."

"I'm on it." I downed the glass of champagne and handed the flute back to Finn. He just shook his head. It was hard to tell if he was amused or exasperated. I'd like to think a little of both. "Keep an eye on laptop girl and try and keep her occupied," I said.

"How would you like me to do that?" Finn asked.

"You're cute. Flirt with her!"

I walked into the supply room and shut the door quietly

after me. A floor lamp had been left on, casting the room in warm light. I stared around at the workroom, looking for Melanie's laptop, my eyes landing on the working industrial printer instead. I walked over and looked at the glossy sheets that were being outputted. Each 11 x 17 sheet had a picture of a painting with text next to it. The two painted rectangles seemed to contrast one another and yet still blended in with the background. Rothko was a master of color. I leaned closer to read one of the descriptions next to the paintings.

Rothko is a pinnacle example of abstract expressionism. His works Untitled (Yellow, Orange, Yellow, Light Orange) from 1955, as well as Untitled, 1970, both attracted some of the larger prices seen at the recent high-profile New York auction. This prestigious sale sent headlines around the art world when Untitled from 1955 sold for 36.5 million dollars, far higher than initially predicted, underlining how the investment side of the art world is in exceptional health at the moment.

This piece No. 20 is a prime example of what Rothko called the "inner light," a quality of luminosity that suggested vivid depths. The painting itself holds its own meaning.

A small stack of completed catalogs sat on the counter behind the printer. Thick white envelopes with hand-scrawled addresses were waiting to be filled. I looked at one of the names and thought it was familiar. I took my phone out and quickly scrolled through my camera roll until I came to a picture of one of the notecards I found in Melanie's desk drawer. The address was a perfect match. The girl who had taken the laptop must've known about the secret compartment in Melanie's drawer as well. The question was, why was Melanie providing the art gallery with addresses? Could it be that the gallery was just looking to target the right clientele or was something more sinister going on?

I picked up the completed catalog and thumbed through it, noting the works of Max Ernst and Heinrich Campendonk. Artists who were slightly less popular, but I had a feeling that was by design. The catalog didn't explicitly state it, but I assumed these were paintings the gallery had procured and were now available for purchase.

Someone walked in and I quickly tucked the catalog down the front of my pants, using my flowy shirt to cover it.

"I'm sorry. I was looking for the restroom, but I walked in here by mistake," I said as I came face-to-face with the laptop snatcher.

The woman glared at me, not believing what I had said for a second.

"You need to start minding your own business." Her accent was as thick as the ice in Siberia.

"I'm afraid I don't know what you're talking about," I said.

"Whatever you're thinking, it's incorrect," she said.

"Really? Because what I'm thinking is that Melanie gave you her client's contact information for you to target. Why, I'm not sure. Blackmail?"

The term evil eye was created for situations like this. I could feel the hate radiating off this woman.

"Or maybe I'm talking to the wrong person. Is Viktor around?" I asked. Did I mention how much this case was starting to irk me? I wasn't playing around.

"My father has nothing to do with this," the woman practically spat at me.

"Your father? You mean Melanie's father."

"It is the same," she said.

"Your Melanie's sister?"

"Half-sister. That's all I'll claim her as."

Wow, talk about cold. Maybe I found myself a new murder suspect. "Why are you so sure of your father's innocence?"

"Because I know his anger. The way he acts now. He will not settle until there is justice."

"Neither will I," I said matter-of-factly.

"Then know this, nothing that is going on here has to do with her death. I promise you that."

I held the woman's gaze, unsure if I believed her or not.

The woman turned and walked back to the door, holding it open for me to exit. I did, quickly.

"Let's go," I said, catching up to Finn. I grabbed him by the arm and headed for the exit. Finn attempted to grab another lobster toast, but I steered him toward the doors instead.

"Hey, a two-second delay wouldn't have killed us," Finn said when we made it outside.

"I'm not too sure about that." I hailed us a cab. "What happened with you flirting with Laptop Girl? I asked Finn as we climbed into our ride.

"Apparently I'm not as hot as you think."

"I wish you would've done something. She totally just busted me. I'm sure I'll be on her radar now."

"What did she say?" Finn asked.

"Other than she's Melanie's sister and I need to mind my own business? Not much."

"I didn't know she had a sister," Finn said.

"Either did I. Technically she's her half-sister. They have the same father and she made sure to emphasize the half part." I then went on to tell Finn about finding the catalog along with the names.

"Melanie was providing her client's names to her sister. Why?" Finn asked.

"That's the question. I have a loose theory, but I'm not going to think it to death. I might be totally wrong. I need to get ahold of Mrs. J."

"Mrs. J.?"

"Her niece is an art history professor at SCAD. I want to have her take a look at this catalog and confirm if I'm on the right track or not." Besides, I needed to call Mrs. J. anyway and talk some wedding details. I had a favor to ask her.

17

I had to wait until the next morning to call Mrs. J., forgetting that it was already after 11 PM in Port Haven. Mrs. J. would chew my ear off if I called her after 9 PM and someone hadn't died. Let me clarify that: someone that she knew hadn't died.

At our hotel room, I used the app on my cell phone to take pictures of the catalog and convert it to a PDF that I could email to Mrs. J's niece, Tasha. Sometimes I loved technology. Mrs. J. was more than willing to help out when I gave her a call.

"This is for a case, isn't it?" Mrs. J. said when I asked for Tasha's phone number. I wanted to speak with her before shooting the email off.

"That it is," I said.

"Oh, girl, you can't even go on vacation without stepping into something," she said.

"You know it," which reminded me to check my email and see if Izzy had sent me that positive energy ritual.

"I know my Tash will help you in heartbeat. Let me get her number for you."

"Thanks, Mrs. J."

Mrs. J. came back on the phone and read off the information I was looking for.

"I have another reason for calling." I had to tread carefully here because once Mrs. J. knew what I was up to, so would the entire town of Port Haven. "What's your schedule look like next weekend? I have a favor to ask."

Mrs. J. was down with my secret wedding plans even if she didn't know exactly what she was agreeing to. I kept it vague on purpose. She had also been right, Tasha jumped at the chance to give me a hand. "Aunt Birdie's always going on about your *super sleuthing skills*, as she calls them."

"Well, I don't know how super they are, but thank you. I'm hoping you can give me a hand with this case. There's a gallery out here called Studio One. I came across a catalog of theirs and I want you to take a look at it and tell me if anything jumps out at you." I left it at that, not wanting my suspicions to influence Tasha.

"No problem. Send it to me and I'll look at it between classes."

"That would be awesome. I'll email it in a minute," I said.

~

WHILE I WAITED for Tasha to get back with me, I got ready for my business meeting with the Senses' executives and called Aria to have valet pull the Mercedes around. I swear I was driving the car more than Aria was. I should've offered to split the rental with her, and I was going to, even though she would've never accepted a penny.

My drive over to Senses was uneventful. It's when I walked into the building that things got interesting. As I stepped into Senses' circular roundabout door I saw Veronica exit the spa. The urge to stay in and follow the door around and exit back out to see where she was going was strong. Veronica was up to something shady. I was positive of it. Her actions did not match up to a grieving mother. There was definitely more going on there.

All throughout my meeting with the Senses executives, which went awesome by the way, I kept thinking about Veronica. She was supposedly suing her daughter, but yet heartbroken over her death. She publicly blamed her daughter's fiancé for her murder, and also made accusations about Zane being jealous, but never backed those claims up. As far as I could tell, dancing didn't pay the bills. And she just dropped $800 on a mid-century typewriter. Unless she was into restoring old typewriters and flipping them for some serious cash, I was at a loss as to what she could be doing to support the lifestyle it was apparent she enjoyed living. All I kept thinking was she had to be working with Viktor somehow. As soon as Tasha called me back I'd be able to know if the idea that had been forming in my head was totally ludicrous or entirely possible. However, even if I understood what was going down between Veronica and Viktor at Studio One, it didn't it still didn't explain who killed Melanie and why.

Irene called me back while I was navigating through downtown traffic. "Hey, just real quick. When did you set up camp there?" I asked.

"Bright and early Thursday morning. We pulled into the camp just before sunrise and I set everything up. Eileen drove the last half of the trip. I let her take a nap while I set things up. In fact, we didn't leave camp at all Thursday, taking a day to recover from the cross-country trek."

"And you never saw anything suspicious or anyone else nearby where Melanie's body was found?"

"Not a thing. You guys were the only people we saw that entire day."

I suspected as much. Melanie must have been murdered sometime in the middle of the night or in the very early hours of Thursday morning. Irene's story seemed to corroborate that.

"Okay, awesome. That's all I needed to know. Thank you!" I hung up with Irene and steered the car in a new direction. It was time to find out where Veronica was Wednesday night.

~

I KNOCKED on Veronica's door and took a step back to see if she would answer. Mitsi was at least home. The Yorkie went into overdrive at the sound of my knocking. Veronica answered a moment later, wearing a fluffy pink robe and with her short hair sticking out in clumps every which way. A silk nightgown skimmed her ankles. She looked night and day from how she had been a couple of hours ago.

Unless the day had worn her out.

"Hi, Ziva. I'm sorry, but I'm not much up for company at the moment," she said, Mitsi wiggling in her arms.

"I met Melanie's sister," I replied.

"What did Sasha have to say?" Veronica looked leery.

I went with the truth. "That I needed to mind my own business."

"Sasha, she's a piece." Veronica held the door open for me to come in. We walked down the foyer and into the kitchen. Veronica put the puppy out and I looked around the room, stopping at the stacked boxes of tea on the counter. Veronica was drinking coffee. I don't know why I found that strange, but I did. I knew it was a clue somehow.

"Coffee?" Veronica offered.

"Um, sure, I'll take a cup."

Interviewing suspects would be so much more enjoyable if I actually enjoyed drinking coffee. Why couldn't people offer me chocolate whenever I stopped by? I had a mental picture of trying to squeeze into my dream gown. Perhaps it was a good thing that they did not.

"What's Sasha's deal? Should I consider her a suspect?" I asked Veronica.

"Sasha hates everyone. Don't take her attitude personally. Plus, she worships the ground her father walks on and thinks everyone else should too."

"But Melanie didn't," I said as a statement.

"No. She was always a bit of a rebel, not that I blamed her. Viktor can be a bit overbearing. That's why I never married him."

"But you have a relationship with him?" I asked.

"When I want to," Veronica replied.

I left it at that.

"Any idea where he was Wednesday night?" I asked.

"We were together at The Met for the opening of the Rodin exhibit. In fact, he was with me when they called about Melanie." The Met was in New York City, which meant neither Veronica nor Viktor had directly killed their daughter. Obviously, they could've still hired someone to, a thought I hadn't speculated much on.

"What about Sasha? Where was she?" I asked.

"Moscow." Veronica poured more coffee into her mug.

Well, that put an end to that.

"Does Zane have an alibi?" Veronica asked me.

"He doesn't," I said.

"What do you make of that?"

"I'm not sure. He's a complex sort of fellow," I replied.

"Just make sure you're looking into him as closely as you're looking at me." Veronica held my gaze over the edge of her coffee cup. I'd be lying if I said I didn't squirm a bit.

"I will." With that nice little threat, I thanked Veronica for her time and left her to her coffee.

~

GETTING BACK IN THE CAR, I thought about what Veronica had just said. Did I need to take a closer look at Zane? And how would I go about doing that? I wasn't convinced I should bother.

Sometimes I do my best thinking in the car and today was no exception. Instead of hitting the glitz and glam of the Strip, I followed my instincts and drove back to the storage unit Veronica visited yesterday. Just as I expected, the gate required a code to open. Unless I came up with the correct code, I'd be stuck on this side of the fence for the time being. I backed up from the gate and drove to the other side of the parking lot to think things through. As I sat there debating my best move forward, Viktor drove into the parking lot. His black Cadillac drove right past me, giving me a clear shot of the driver.

I was wrong. They weren't using the gated self-storage unit around back, but rather the available inside storage. I re-read the storage company's sign. Below the company's name were the words "climate-controlled solutions." The concept never occurred to me, but it should have. I imagined the heat would destroy several personal belongs if they were left to the fate of the elements. I parked at the other end of the strip mall in front of a thrift store and watched

Viktor from afar. He was a portly sort of fellow. I saw that clearly now as he as he heaved himself out of the car and took a minute to regain his balance. Equilibrium in check, he began to waddle toward the storage building. The image of him reminded me of one of the Tweedle Twins from Alice in Wonderland, minus the yellow-flagged baseball cap.

This time, I was going in. As far as I knew, Viktor didn't know who I was. Even if Sasha or Veronica had told him about me, I was yet to meet his acquaintance. I was planning on keeping it that way.

I gave Viktor a five-minute head start and then walked in the building after him. Inside was much like how a storage unit looked outside. Rows and rows of rolled down doors and lockers in various sizes. Some of the units were as wide as a single-car garage. Others were the width of a regular-sized door. And yet others were small lockers, stacked on top of one another. The floors were glossy concrete, the bolts padlocked, and the lighting, fluorescent. My heels clicked on the concrete, echoing down the hall. I waved hi at the first man I passed. He was using a furniture dolly to load concession equipment into his unit. I'd recognized a cotton candy machine anywhere.

"Excuse me," I said, dashing in front of him as he attempted to maneuver the machine backwards into his space. The concession man tipped his hat to me in a polite gesture. I thought it was a shame that not everyone had such nice manners these days.

At the end of the hall, I debated which way to go, right or left? The sound of someone speaking Russian had me turning left. It sounded as if Viktor was talking on his phone. What he was saying I obviously had no clue and I didn't think Google translate would work from that far away.

I decided to play it cool and just casually walk by his storage unit, pretend I was on a mission to someplace else. As I walked by, I turned my head ever so slightly and casted a glance inside.

The side wall of the unit contained slotted storage with wrapped parcels tucked between each slot. Paintings, I surmised. Off-site storage for the gallery. But then I caught sight of a filing cabinet with another table set up to the side of it. A workstation with Veronica's newly purchased typewriter set on it. What was that about?

Viktor hung up his phone and caught my eye. I quickly looked away and continued down the hall.

"Miss? Miss!" Viktor called after me. "MISS!" he commanded.

I froze.

Running would make me look guilty. I was torn as to what I should do. Flight usually kicked in, but today, fight did. I was ready to have it out, here and now. Demand some answers. I whipped around, ready for a showdown.

"Can you confirm the humidity is set at forty-five percent?" Viktor asked me.

It took me a second to realize Viktor thought I worked there. The pencil skirt and high heels probably gave that impression.

"Yes. Let me double-check and I'll get right back with you," I said, turning and marching toward where I assumed the front offices were located.

I may have started marching too fast because I swore at that moment Viktor started following me. *Don't look back*, I told myself. *Keep your eyes forward.* Click, click, click, my heels echoed. Squeak, squeak, squeak, went the rubber-soled shoes behind me.

The person's breathing sounded heavy, just as I imagined Viktor's would if he attempted to catch up to me. I couldn't help it. I looked over my shoulder and crashed right into the man with the concession unit. Only this time he was exiting with the slushie machine. Gallons of blue raspberry syrup flew off the dolly and cracked onto the floor. My heel caught in the sticky mess and took me down with it.

OOOF! I could feel the sugary goo seep through my shirt and down the back of my legs.

"Ma'am, let me help you up!" the concession man said. I took his hand and allowed him to help peel me off the floor.

"I'll go get some help," said the younger teenage boy who had turned out to be the one following me. He set down the television he had been carrying and ran toward the front offices.

"I'm fine, really," I said, eager now more than ever to get out there. "Let me dash into the bathroom to get cleaned up and I'll grab some paper towels to take care of this mess," I said. The concession man bent down and started to re-stack the dolly and I popped off my heels and walked down the rest of the hall, around the corner, and out the door before anyone else could stop me.

18

"Can you bring me down some clothes?" I asked Finn as I pulled up to the hotel.

"Say what?" Finn yelled into his phone.

"Syrup incident." I took two seconds in the storage unit's parking lot to debate stripping down or not. In the end, respect for the Mercedes and Aria won out. "I'm out front and hurry up. I can't keep waving the valet away."

My hair still smelled faintly of blue raspberry, and my face had a stubborn blue splatter on it, but it blended in nicely with the cuts, so all-in-all I was only slightly a hot mess.

"What are you up to?" I asked Finn while I towel dried my hair. He was sitting cross-legged on the bed. My laptop resting on his legs.

"Hacking into Melanie's email," he replied. Not even looking up.

"Wait, what?!" I dropped the towel.

"Turns out you can in fact learn everything online."

"I thought we'd have to manually install spyware or pay your buddy big bucks to do that," I said.

"Not to hack email. I've learned that it's freakishly easy to do."

I saddled up next to Finn on the bed. "What have you found out?" I asked.

"Nothing Earth shattering. Here, take a look." Finn turned the computer for me to see.

He was right, there wasn't much to look at. "Go to the next page." Together we scrolled down the list. Coupons, forwards, industry newsletters, conference details.

"What about that one?" I pointed to the last message on the screen titled "Contract."

SEE ATTACHED for the latest contract sent over. I said you'd take a look at it.

-Lee

"WHO IN THE WORLD IS LEE?" I asked Finn.

Finn clicked on the contact list and saw the sender's full name was Lee Strauss. A quick Google search told us he was a local business attorney.

"Click on the attachment and see what it says," I said. We were doing just that when there was a knock on the door. I temporarily forgot about my disastrous state and opened it.

Aria looked shocked. Vince looked slightly amused.

"Sharpie accident" I said by way of explaining the blue on my face. Aria knew that was a load of baloney.

"The pen is blue," Vince said with a smile on his face, quoting Jim Carey.

"Exactly," I said. Now had they seen me thirty minutes

before I showered the rest of the syrup away, it would've been harder to explain.

"Are you still okay with going tonight?" Aria asked me.

"Tonight? What's tonight?" I asked.

"Sorry, I forgot to tell her. Vince booked us the VIP experience at Cirque du Soleil. We don't have to go," Finn said, shutting the laptop.

"Which one is it?" I asked.

"The Beatles LOVE," Vince replied.

"Of course. I'm not surprised." I looked over at Finn. He loved the Beatles. True story.

"What time's the show?" I asked.

"It's at 9:30. We were going to grab dinner beforehand," Aria said, still trying to get a read on me.

"I'm down with that. Aria, come help me pick something out to wear. Why don't you guys have a pre-dinner drink," I said to Finn.

"I think I'm going to need a pre-dinner drink," Aria said under her breath to me.

Aria followed me out of the living room and around the corner to the master suite.

"Sharpie accident?" she asked me incredulously.

"Okay, so I had a run-in with a slushie machine while doing some recon work, but don't worry, the Mercedes is clean." Aria eyes went wide. Of course, that statement lead to further explanation.

When I was done, Aria said, "So, he's storing artwork at the unit? That's not surprising."

"The typewriter too. Not storing it, but working on it. That's important, I just don't know why. Now seriously, help me find something to wear," I said.

I love getting dressed up. I seriously do. Especially when I'm hitting the town with my best friend and our hot dates.

Finn dressed up is even hotter than Finn dressed down. He wore a pair of gray dress pants with a light blue shirt opened at the collar just enough. Black dress shoes and a black buckle were the only accessories the man needed. I had gone for a high-necked short black dress. I twisted my hair up and chose a pair of long sparkly earrings to distract from my blue-speckled and scratched-up face. My years as a Beauty Secrets Representative had served me well. I stared at my reflection and could barely notice the speckles or scratches. The look seemed to work on Finn anyway.

"You look amazing," he said.

"As do you. You guys ready to go?" I asked.

CIRQUE DU SOLEIL is an experience right from the moment you arrive. The costumes and sounds, the music and performers, they all make you take a step back and say, wow! And that was only during the pre-show. Our tickets included a reception where we could mingle with other VIP guests and performers before the show.

"Hi, welcome to LOVE. We're excited to have you here." The performer's face was painted in shades of blue with crystals circling his eyes. The color matched his wide-striped bodysuit and fur coat. A silver-sequined top hat completed the look. I felt underdressed once more and certain that no one would notice my mess of a face.

"First show?" he asked us.

"For me, but I'm pretty sure these two have been to several," I motioned to Aria and Vince, letting them take over the conversation.

"How about I grab us a couple drinks?" Finn offered.

"Sounds good, babe. Thanks." I turned from Aria and

Vince and surveyed the room, taking in all the intricate details of the performers' costumes. The colors and textures were amazing. From the fabric-draped walls to the delectable hors d'oeuvres being served, everything had a certain flare to it. I could clearly see the overlap between Mr. Frederick's designs and the theater. In fact, I saw the same mint-green floral print of one of his dresses on one of the performers. I started to wonder why Mr. Frederick left the theater. The bright patterns and bold colors seemed to match his style manifesto.

The lights flickered above about the same time Finn returned and we moved off to find our seats.

For almost an hour I was able to sit back, relax, and enjoy the glitz and glamour Vegas was supposed to be. Cirque du Soleil was said to amaze and it did. The imagery of sound was so superb that at times I was left speechless. The mashed-up Beatles music was inspiring and the acts entrancing. The costuming, special effects, and set design were mesmerizing. Talk about witnessing a revolution well, a fantasy revolution, courtesy of the Beatles.

When intermission came around it took me a second to realize what was going on.

"Break time," Finn said.

"The show's fantastic," I said, surprised by how much I had enjoyed the first half.

A private balcony and bathroom came with our show's tickets, so we all headed that way for some fresh air.

"Where'd the guys go?" I asked Aria when I realized they weren't behind us.

Aria pointed across the room. Vince appeared to be talking to his doppelgänger about business, no doubt, and Finn was talking to a man dressed in silver with a tea cup glued to the side of his head. We left them to their conversations.

"Look at her costume. I love it." It was a red-laced and pearled bodice with shimmery built-in iridescent wings that appeared whenever she fluttered her arms. The woman walked right toward us, so I took it as an opportunity to tell her so.

"Your costume is gorgeous," I said to her.

"Thank you so much. It's one of my favorites." She fluttered her wings for added emphasis.

"That is beautiful," Aria added.

"I'll have to let my uncle know. He designed it." It's not every day that you get to meet the person that you had just impersonated a couple days before. Today was my lucky day.

"Does your uncle happened to be Paul Frederick?" I asked.

"The one and only. I'm going to miss working with him on these designs. Now that he's obsessed with bridal, I don't think he's ever going to come back to theater."

"Why the switch? This costume seems so much like his personality," I said.

"He said he lost his muse and found it again with bridal. I've learned that you can't argue with a creative genius."

"I guess that's true," Aria said.

"He's probably having a nervous breakdown after Melanie's death," Taylor added.

I found that comment hard to believe. "I didn't think the two were close. In fact, I heard they had a bit of a rivalry going on."

Taylor waved my comment away. "No, they reconciled a while ago. It was more the industry trying to hype up something that it wasn't there. In fact, he just told me about a joint venture they were working on, a new label. Culture for the masses."

"Wait, she had a joint venture planned?" Neither Gwen nor Clarissa mentioned anything, but then again maybe they didn't know about it. Gwen had said she stayed more into the design side of things. As for Clarissa, I didn't see how being the store manager made her privy to Mr. Frederick's business dealings.

"I have no idea what's going to happen to the label now," Gwen said.

"Have you talked with your uncle?" Aria asked.

"No, but that's the norm. He's really good at unplugging." Aria went on to say something about how good it was to do that every now and then. I wouldn't know. I was too addicted to technology to take a break, which probably meant that I should.

Taylor left us to get back to the show and the wheels in my head started spinning. Who wouldn't have wanted Melanie partnering up with Mr. Frederick? Victor and Veronica were number one and two on my list. I was also thinking this was exactly why Melanie had found the courage to tell her dad to stuff it. The more financially independent she became, the less she needed his money. No money meant no control. I needed to get back to the hotel room and read that attachment to confirm, but I was betting that contract in Melanie's email was between her and Mr. Frederick. I had to get back to the hotel and read it.

~

I INTERRUPTED Finn's conversation with the performer to tell him I was taking off. "I'll come with you," he said after I explained why.

"No, stay. You're really into the show." I knew that if I had enjoyed it, he was in heaven.

"But—"

"Don't worry about me. I'm going right back to the hotel. Promise. I want to check out a couple of things online."

"It's late."

"Is it ever late in Vegas?" I countered.

"Good point."

"I'll text you when I'm back in our room." I kissed Finn on the cheek. "With any luck, I'll have this case cracked by the time you get back."

Didn't I say I was the ever optimist?

19

I was right about one thing. It was never late in Vegas. Crowds gathered around the Bellagio's dazzling fountains as they performed their awe-inspiring water ballet. I slowed my pace ever so slightly to watch it myself.

Next to me, a man turned a chunk of the sidewalk into a three-dimensional work of art. It looked as if the buildings were coming right up out of the ground.

My phone buzzed in my purse and I stopped to check it out. A move that almost cost me my life. It was a text message with one word: *Goodbye.*

"Goodbye? What in the world?" I looked at the number to see who it was from and didn't see the lights drive up behind me.

"Hey! Watch out!" Another woman shouted to me.

I turned to see a set of wheels hop the curb and a car came racing toward me. Stunned, I stood there frozen, staring down the grill of a car that was set on running me over. Honda. That was the last thought I had before a man pushed me out of the way. My head smacked the cement and the lights went out.

I WOKE up in the hospital. It turned out Finn was that man who had pushed me out of the way. Beatles fanatic or not, he told me he didn't like the thought of me walking back to the hotel alone. Turns out he was right to be worried.

"Sweet, sweet, sugar," I said, touching the bump on my head. "Somebody get me some chocolate." My eyes came into focus and I saw Aria and Finn at my side, a mixture of smiles and tears on their faces.

"What in the world happened?" Even as I said the words I had visions of a car's headlights shinning in my eyes before total darkness.

"Hit the nurse light and let them know she's awake," Vince said. I noticed him for the first time, sitting in the side chair, chewing on his nails.

I tried to slowly sit up. The throbbing in my head kept me down. "Was anyone else hurt?" I asked.

"No, the driver seemed to take aim just at you," Finn said.

"What do you mean seemed? Didn't they catch them?" The look on everyone's faces told me they didn't.

"But they used the video footage from the Strip to track the car to the Fremont garage," Vince said, getting up and coming to stand by Aria.

"It was a Honda, right?" I thought of the emblem that came racing toward me.

"It was," Aria said.

I thought of something else at that moment. "It was someone who had my number. They texted me right before running me down." I looked around for my phone, but I had no idea where it was.

"Who have you given your card out to?" Aria asked. Finn searched in the plastic bag next to my bed and pulled out my phone.

I tried to think, but it made my head hurt. Who hadn't I given it out too? "Detective Hart, Shelly the reporter, Gwen at Melanie's boutique, Clarissa at Paul Frederick's, Melanie's mom and her sister. Not to mention the hundreds of people at the conference." A stack of my business cards had been provided to the attendees along with my branding handout.

"I'm not comfortable with any of this," Vince said, interrupting my brain storming. I stopped and looked up at him. He was more of a nervous wreck than all of the rest of us combined.

"I don't blame you. I wouldn't be comfortable with any of this either," I said.

"The conference is over. I think we should go home," he said.

"I'm not leaving just yet," I said to Finn. Finn nodded, knowing it would be pointless to argue. "Before you go back home, can I talk to Aria for a minute, alone?" I needed her help if I was going to pull my master plan off. Hopefully she'd be game.

~

THE HOSPITAL KEPT me overnight for observation, releasing me the next morning after I passed a neurological evaluation and had a clean CT scan. By that time Aria and Vince were on their way back to Port Haven. Although Aria had a very special task at hand that she was thrilled to take on.

"Did you hear back from Tasha?" Finn asked me as I laid comfortably in bed back at the hotel.

"No." In fact, I hadn't heard back from Tasha or Irene. I was starting to lose hope. If we couldn't put the pieces together with what information we had, then we were in trouble.

Just as I was about to tell Finn that we might as well keep our evening flight, my phone rang. It was Tasha.

"Sorry, it took me longer to get back with you than I'd like. I wanted to double-check that I was right before calling you back," she said.

"What did you find out?" I asked, sitting up in bed.

"All of the paintings in the catalog are previously unknown works. I'm sure of it."

"What does that mean exactly?" I asked.

"It means that somehow this art dealer of yours has either received an unbelievable windfall or he's peddling forged works. Did he say how he'd come by the pieces?"

"I haven't had a chance to ask for an explanation yet," I said.

"You might want to, or better yet, call the FBI. This has art crime written all over it." I wasn't sure about calling the FBI, but Detective Hart was supposed to stop by in a little bit.

20

While Finn caught up on some sleep, I spent that time researching art crimes and how galleries like Studio One fit into the scheme. By the time Detective Hart knocked on my door, things were starting to make sense.

"Come on in," I said. For the first time in twenty-four hours I was wearing pants— well, if leggings counted as pants—and was even sporting some lipstick and eyeliner. I didn't bother covering the bruise on the side of my face. Purple was always my color.

"Let's have a seat over here." I motioned to the sofa and side chair. My laptop sat in front of me on the coffee table. Finn was still asleep down the hall in the master.

I handed the catalog over to Detective Hart once she was seated.

"I had my professor friend take a look at that. None of the pieces in this catalog are previously known. She told me that either Viktor is extremely lucky or..."

"He's peddling forged works," Detective Hart said.

"Exactly. I also found notecards in Melanie's desk drawer

that match the addresses on the envelopes the gallery was mailing the catalogs out to."

"You were in her office?" Detective Hart wasn't sure if she should be upset or impressed.

I waved her comment away. The details were irrelevant. I brought up the photos on my phone and showed Detective Hart the matching addresses and the notecards.

"There was also a notebook, with a series of numbers. I think the first digits are phone numbers, followed by store account numbers or maybe how much money they spent. I'm not positive," I said. It was the best theory I had.

"A notebook?" Detective Hart asked. I showed her a couple other pictures.

"Oh, and Veronica just bought an $800 mid-century typewriter," I said, if that explained it all.

"I'm not following."

"Well, I did a bit of research. It looks like forging a painting is only the first part. You also need fake documents, you know, letters and receipts, provenance they call it, to provide authenticity. If you're peddling mid-century paintings, you need mid-century provenance, which also explains all the tea boxes!" I stood up, officially on a roll.

"Tea boxes?"

"On Veronica's counter. I was at her house and she offered me coffee, twice. I found it strange seeing she had boxes of tea sitting out, but now it makes sense."

"Still not following," Detective Hart said.

I turned my computer Detective Hart's way to the tutorial I had been reading online when she had knocked on the door. "Forgers use tea to stain paper. Makes it look older. That must be what she's doing. If you can get a warrant for their storage unit, I bet the pieces will really click together."

"Storage unit?" Detective Hart asked.

I told the detective all about Viktor and Veronica's storage unit, including where it was located and what was inside.

"Did I tell you about Veronica's lawsuit?" I asked Detective Hart.

"No, but that my team did uncover."

"I'm thinking that Veronica was blackmailing Melanie. Trying to force her into staying with the operation, but it seems she had gone rogue."

"Who killed Melanie then?" Detective Hart asked.

I sat back down. My roll had come to an end. "I have no idea. Common sense would say Veronica, but I don't have any evidence to back that up, just speculation." It looked like I had solved one crime, but still was clueless when it came to solving Melanie's murder. It appeared Melanie's sister might have been correct. Whatever they were up to at Studio One, it had nothing to do with Melanie's murder. Talk about an anticlimactic ending.

"Do you have any idea?" I asked Detective Hart.

"As far as I'm concerned, any one of her family members could have done it. They all appear to have a motive," she said.

"That's true, I guess. What about the car that hit me, did you trace it?" I asked.

"That's where it gets sticky. The car was registered to Lucia," Detective Hart said.

"Lucia? The murders are connected?" This really started the wheels spinning in my head.

"Looks that way, but I have no idea how. I'm going to get in touch with the FBI." Detective Hart held up the catalog. "This might not be the type of quick-close case you're used to, but I know we'll crack it eventually."

I nodded my head, still not feeling the type of closure I was hoping for.

Detective Hart stood up. "I wish you well, Ziva. You're one heck of a detective. Take care and I'm sure I'll be in touch."

"Thanks, please do." I walked Detective Hart out and stood at the small kitchenette counter.

I thought back to Melanie's sister statement for the hundredth time. What if the murders were entirely separate from the art crimes? What if we removed Veronica, Viktor, and Sasha as suspects. Who did that leave?

My cell phone rang at that moment. It was a number that I vaguely recognized. I answered the line anyway.

"Hey Ziva. It's Clarissa."

"Oh hey, how's it going?"

"Crazy busy here, but I wanted to let you know that Mr. Frederick's back in town. He stopped in this morning."

"Oh awesome. Did you tell him to call me?"

"I did, but I'm don't think he was listening. He said Belize left him inspired and he's heading to the fabric warehouse to work."

"Fabric warehouse?"

"It's the old Sears building off of 95. He bought it on a deal and says the lighting inside is fabulous."

"Okay, cool. Thanks so much."

~

I SNUCK out of the hotel room and had the valet hail me a cab. "Old Sears building on I-95," I said to the driver, unsure if he knew what I was talking about or not. The cabbie nodded, which I assumed meant he did.

"Are you being smart or stupid?" I asked myself as the

cab drove down I-95. Smart people called the police, stupid people raced off to abandoned warehouses. I had to back my thoughts up. Did I think Mr. Frederick was a murderer? No, no I did not. Because it didn't make sense for him to firebomb his own apartment. If anything, being anywhere near his vicinity was more of a danger than the man himself. I could only hope that the person who was after him didn't know he was in town yet. Speaking of being firebombed, I needed to talk to Mr. Frederick and find out if he knew who was after him and why.

The Sears building was at one end of a mall, so not nearly the creepy abandoned warehouse I had been expecting. One point for the smart column, or maybe I should create another column titled "dumb luck."

I walked up to the sliding glass doors and gave a little jump back when they automatically opened. I was not expecting that to happen. In fact, the whole building defied expectations. This wasn't some abandoned warehouse, but more like a fashion factory. Rows upon rows of fabric took up the front portion of the store with designers walking about choosing material to work with. On the other side, I could see other designers happily pinning at their workstations. Mannequins draped in swatches of fabric this way and that. I planned on walking around and exploring to see what other oddities I could find until security stopped me.

"Can I help you ma'am?"

So apparently you couldn't just waltz in here and look around.

"Hi, I was just wondering if Mr. Frederick was available?" I asked the man. I'm sure he's going to want to talk with me when he finds out who I am," I said more confidently than I felt.

"And who might that be?"

"Ziva Diaz." I let my name hang in the air like a total boss babe would.

My gamble paid off. Either I was more popular than I thought I was, or Mr. Frederick had been listening when Clarissa told him I was trying to get in touch.

"Ziva, my peach, I've heard wonderful things about you." Mr. Frederick came out from a back office, wearing a white suit. A silver shimmering cape flowed behind him.

"I know what it's like when your muse strikes, but do you have a minute to chat?" I asked him.

"That I can do, come this way," the man said.

Mr. Frederick's office was bathed in natural light and all things white. The furniture, walls, fabric. There wasn't a drop of color in sight. It was blinding.

Mr. Frederick picked up a white pencil and sat at his desk, ready to take notes on a white piece of paper.

"I heard about your apartment. I'm so sorry. Any idea who did it?" I asked.

"No, but it's concerning. Very concerning. I'd drive myself crazy if I tried to make sense of it all."

"That's true, but I can't help but think it's connected to Melanie's murder. Don't you think so too?"

"Melanie's murder? Why in the world would it be?" The thought seemed to have seriously never crossed his mind.

I tried a different approach. "You and Melanie were set to go into business together, is that right?"

"We were. This time it was going to be glorious. A vision. I couldn't wait to explore the world of bridal with Ms. May." I swear Mr. Frederick's eyes got all misty when he talked about it.

"This time? Was there a time before?" I asked.

"There was, but I let a foolish sketchbook get in the way."

"The one that was stolen, right?" Mr. Frederick looked surprised. "Industry gossip," I supplied.

"Yes, that notebook. I was convinced Melanie stole it when I saw her work and the rumors swirled. I didn't want to believe there was another designer as talented as me."

"You were too proud," I said.

"I was, but Melanie came to me. We talked everything out and I grew up."

"Is it possible that there's someone who would've wanted to wipe the two of you out? A rival?"

"No, no. Not possible. No one else knew about our planned label."

"Are you sure? Your niece is the one who told me about it," I said.

"Okay, no one else knew but her. I forgot about that. Isn't Taylor just wonderful? I love that girl."

"What about your lawyers?" I asked.

"What lawyers?"

"Wait, you two didn't sign a contract last month?"

"Last month? No. We just met Tuesday morning."

"But wait, I saw a contract." I reached for my phone to bring up the email only to realize it was on my computer.

"Not for us. Our label never got that far. I never even had a chance to call my lawyer."

"Then who in the world is the contract between?

"Me." I jumped in my seat and turned around to face Gwen. With a blowtorch in one hand, a lighter in the other, and a whole lot of crazy in her eyes, the woman commanded respect. Too bad I was a little low on it.

"Sweet sugar! What in the world are you thinking?" I asked her. Mr. Frederick looked around the room trying to figure out what was going on. Gwen lit the torch and walked over to a rack of lace, lighting the ends on fire. They curled instantly in the heat.

She smiled. "No one ever took Gwen seriously, did they? What about now? Do you take me seriously?" Gwen pointed the blowtorch in our faces. I held completely still while my mind put the pieces together.

"You were getting cut out, weren't you? You wanted to go into business with Melanie, but she turned to Mr. Frederick instead."

"We had a deal. She promised me that if her name was on the label, she would make me partner once the brand took off. Well, the brand took off, and there I was, still a designer."

"And her family?" I asked.

"I knew she wanted out of their control, so I gave her a way out. Together we had the finances to go in alone and cut her father out of the business, and she agreed to it. That is until this fruit loop came along."

Gwen played the torch across Mr. Frederick's white desk. Whatever the furniture had been lacquered with, it went up in flames. I jumped back.

"I got rid of you once, but you just kept coming back," she said to Mr. Frederick.

"Got rid of me? But I never went anywhere," Mr. Frederick said.

"The sketchbook. You stole it in Paris and started the rumors about it being Melanie," I said.

"I did and it worked for a while. I should've known you'd be back," Gwen said.

"That was very wrong of you," Mr. Frederick said as if he was scolding a young child. Meanwhile, his desk went up in flames, taking his white pencils and paper along with it.

"I'm tired of my work being insulted and cast aside. I'm

someone!" Gwen shouted. She turned and lit a bolt of white silk. Flames climbed up the fabric. I found myself more interested in the blowtorch at that moment and not so much the burning fabric. I did not want to get singed by the psycho.

Mr. Frederick's desk continued to burn as did the lace and fabric. I looked at the lace and thought to what Gwen had just said.

"You killed Lucia because she rejected your dress."

"She didn't deserve that dress or the lace I strangled her with," Gwen said, explaining the imprint Detective Hart found around Lucia's neck.

"Then you killed Melanie. Your text was your alibi, but you didn't send it from home. You used Melanie's phone to reply to yourself. I bet when the police pull your cell records they'll see that your message wasn't transmitted from a tower anywhere near your home." The more I thought of it, the more it made sense. "I'm sure it wasn't hard to get her to go with you. You probably got her drunk when you were out celebrating. Was she even conscious when you bashed in her head?" I asked.

"She deserved it!" Gwen turned the blowtorch on Mr. Frederick's white leather couch.

I was proud to have finally solved the case. It was just too bad we'd all be burned up to a crisp before Detective Hart would ever know.

"My name is supposed to be on the front of the store. Not hers. I'm the designer!" Gwen shouted once more.

"My child, this is all complete nonsense. Put the blowtorch down and let's talk about your vision," Mr. Frederick looked completely calm. I thought Gwen's reference to him as fruit loop was spot on until I saw the way Gwen responded to him.

"I wanted to use more lace, less tulle. Vintage necklines and crystal beading. No more ridiculous ball gowns and feathers. No crazy colors. Just pure white. Surely you understand my vision?" Gwen was practically begging Mr. Frederick to believe in her.

Mr. Frederick played his part to a T. "That would be splendid to see," he said. As far as I was concerned, the only people Gwen would be designing for were the Nevada State inmates.

"I wanted to make classical dresses for today's bride," Gwen said.

"The classics never go out of style," Mr. Frederick said. I looked around the room as the flames started to spread to the carpeting. For as special as this moment was for Gwen, the smoke was starting to burn my eyes. This had to stop.

"But she ruined it!" Gwen said, stomping her feet. She looked around the room, as if she was trying to see what else she could burn. I didn't give her that chance. The moment her back was turned from me, I smacked her on the back with a chair, cage fighting-style.

The blowtorch rolled from her hands and I had a moment of panic. Go after it or subdue Gwen? Mr. Frederick pounced on Gwen like a feral cat. He sure was springy. I ran for the torch and twisted the gas off just as the flame made contact with the curtains. The gauzy fabric shriveled up in flame. I jumped back, looking around for something, anything, to put out the flames. At that moment, Zane came racing into the room, fire extinguisher in hand, and doused the flames. Leave it to a rock star to save the day.

"How did you know where to find us?" I asked Zane. We

were standing in the mall parking lot. The fire fighters were inside putting out the remaining flames. Gwen was already in police custody.

"I followed Gwen. After I realized Viktor wouldn't kill Melanie, I put my prejudice aside and thought who would? Who had the most to gain? The answer was clear. Gwen. She would inherit the salon, the brand, everything."

"I never even thought of her," I said.

"Melanie thought of her like a sister," Zane said.

With family like that… "So you went to confront her?" I asked.

"And she led me here," Zane said.

"Well I'm glad she did." I gave Zane a hug and wondered in that moment if it would be totally inappropriate to ask for an autograph.

21

In the ideal world, I wouldn't be hopping on a flight five days after crashing a helicopter. But this wasn't an ideal world. I took a deep breath and looked over at my travel companion. Finn was as content as could be, reading the pamphlet that had been tucked in the seat back in front of him, debating his beverage choices. At that moment, I was thinking I should've called my family physician, Dr. Michelson, and had him call in a prescription for Xanax. Beverage service could not start soon enough.

A woman sitting across the aisle from us had a small poodle sitting on her lap that reminded me so much of Captain Jack I felt homesick. I was eternally grateful to be flying back to Port Haven and putting Vegas behind us.

I convinced Finn to spend a couple of days in Port Haven instead of heading directly down to Tampa with the promise that I would accompany him. Both of us were tired of living apart, and I was ready to make the move permanent. That just meant packing up the rest of my apartment and signing a few more papers, oh, and getting married.

"Remember when I said I had a project that needed

some tweaking?" I asked Finn as we packed up the rest of my apartment a few days later.

"Yes?" Finn said, cocking his head and looking at me questioningly.

"Well it's done."

The last thing left in my apartment was an envelope that I had hid on the top of the refrigerator. I climbed up on the counter to retrieve it. Finn watched me curiously the entire time.

"I would cordially like to invite you to our wedding," I said, handing the envelope over.

Finn took the invitation from me, our only wedding invitation, and carefully read it.

"It's tomorrow," he said, a mixture of shock and surprise in his voice.

"It is. You free?" I asked, eyebrows raised, waiting for his response.

"But babe, I don't have anything to wear," Finn joked, but I knew he was somewhat serious.

"Don't worry about that. In fact, Vince has you all taken care of. He should be here any minute to pick you up for a little bachelor party fun and then I'll see you tomorrow evening."

I waited to see how Finn would react. Had I gone too far by keeping everything a secret from him?

Finn picked up and spun me around my now empty kitchen. "I love you, boss babe," he said, giving me a kiss to end all kisses. I guess that answered that.

~

Our wedding cruise took off from the marina. The same place where I had first laid eyes on my shirtless hottie and decided he was a man that I had to meet. It was also where we had our first date and found our first dead body. I'm not sure if that was a point in its favor or not.

Finn once told me that the only thing he loved as much as me was the ocean. Getting married on a sunset cruise as our boat slipped out of the sound was about as perfect as I could've ever dreamed of.

Aria nailed everything, from the bite-sized tuxedo cupcakes, to the lobster toasts and grilled oysters as hors d'oeuvres, and bottles of rosé chilling on ice. Of course, she also had a separate ice chest full of Coca-Cola for Finn, but not just the usual cans; these were the classic glass bottles that no one could resist. The star of the dessert table was our wedding cake, courtesy of none other than Mrs. J. You know how much I loved her world-famous chocolate cake. I would've been content with just a thick slice of that.

Our wedding might have been low country, but it wasn't low style. My look was flawless, Finn's handsome, and with the addition of our closest family and friends, my heart was full.

Now if only I could do something about always finding dead bodies...

BEAUTY & BLOODSHED

BEAUTY SECRETS BOOK 5

Can't a girl get a vacation?

If you're Ziva Diaz, that answer is no. What's worse, no one believes Ziva when she tells them about the attack she just witnessed. Where's the victim? Where's the evidence?
If Ziva could just forget what she saw she could walk away, but images like that never leave you and neither will Ziva, even if that means riding out the hurricane that's heading straight towards the resort.

Can Ziva solve a murder and fly to safety before the storm hits? Or will she be trapped on an island with the killer on the loose? Find out in Book 5 of the Beauty Secrets Series!

Available December 12th

Preorder at: myBook.to/BeautyBloodshed

Beauty & Bloodshed
A Beauty Secrets Mystery
Book Five
STEPHANIE DAMORE

ABOUT THE AUTHOR

I'm a mystery author with a soft spot for romance and humor, too. I love all things girlie with a dollop of danger, have a strong affinity for the color pink (especially in diamonds and champagne), and, not to brag, but chocolate and I are in a pretty serious relationship. My books feature fearless females, a little bit of love, a few laughs, and a whole lot of whodunit. I hope my stories keep you guessing and laughing all the way until the end.

I love my fans! Let's chat!

www.stephaniedamore.com
steph.damore@gmail.com